I0523719

Enter
the World
of
Shadows
and
Mists

Faith Beyond
THE SHADOWS

Book 1 of the Believe Series

Charlene Campfield and Leon Campfield Sr.

**Illustrations and Cover Design
by Charlene Campfield**

CAMPFIELD AND CAMPFIELD
PUBLISHING LLC

Faith Beyond the Shadows is a work of fiction. Names, characters, places, and incidents are either the product of the author's imagination or are used fictitiously. Any resemblance to actual persons, living or dead, events or locales is entirely coincidental.
Copyright © 2009 Charlene M. Campfield and Leon V. Campfield Sr.
Published 2010 by Campfield and Campfield Publishing,
Philadelphia, PA All rights reserved.
www.campfieldspublishing.com
ISBN: 978-0-9817025-6-8 Print
ISBN: 978-0-9817025-7-5 eBook
Library of Congress Control Number 2008910881
FICTION | CHRISTIAN | FUTURISTIC | DYSTOPIAN | TEEN/YA
FIRST EDITION
Illustrations by Charlene Michele Campfield
Cover design by Charlene Michele Campfield
No part of this book may be reproduced or transmitted in any form or by any means, electronic or mechanical, including photocopying, recording, or by any informational storage or retrieval system without permission in writing from the publisher.
Please direct inquires to the permissionseditor@campfieldspublishing,com
Scripture taken from the HOLY BIBLE, NEW INTERNATIONAL VERSION®
Copyright © 1973,1978,1984 by International Bible Society.
Used by permission of Zondervan Publishing House. All rights reserved.
The "NIV" and "New International Version" trademarks are registered in the United States Patent and Trademark Office by International Bible Society. Use of either trademark requires the permission of International Bible Society.

THANK YOU FATHER, FOR ALL THE GIFTS YOU'VE GIVEN US.

"EVERY GOOD AND PERFECT gift is from above, coming down from the Father of the heavenly lights, Who does not change like shifting shadows." James 1:17

Cast of Characters

Love, Joy, Peace, Patience, Kindness, Goodness, Faithfulness, Gentleness, Self-Control - The Cloud People

Angeleigh Aman St. James - 17 Year Old Main Character and Narrator of the Story

Tommy Watchthee - Angeleigh's "little brother" neighbor

Kyra Christian - Angeleigh's best friend

Jamie Christian - Kyra's cousin

Nana - Grandmom who parented Angeleigh

Michael T (Thriambeuo) - Angeleigh's Dad

Holbert Thriambeuo - Angeleigh's Grandfather

Elizabeth St. James - Angeleigh's Mom

Mrs. Charity Woodrow - Angeleigh's Teacher

Lady Maggie - Homeless Woman

Mrs. Maple - Old Woman

Mr. Greeley - Mission caretaker

General Michael Thomas - Head of Biosphere 6

Major Hunt, Colonel Dyer, Lieutenant Calvin Heartley, Private Dauntler, Private Zitman - Employees of Biosphere Six

Dr. Mortimus - Chief Physician of the Cloning Department and Physician General of the New World Court Administration

Nurse Loveless, Nurse Goodman - Other Employees of Biosphere Six

Mr. Killmanski and Mr. Slayman - Guards at Biosphere Six

Horatio - Prisoner at Biosphere Six

Romulus - Guard at Region 22 Mission City Alliance

The Catfish - As the Catfish

TABLE OF CONTENTS

SCRIPTURE VERSE

"Don't be afraid; just believe." Mark 5:36

PROLOGUE

THE YEAR IS 2112. Planet Earth is under New World Court jurisdiction. Twenty-nine regions of the globe are each divided into three zones. Zone A or Biosphere, houses select members of the population for the sole purpose of propagating and passing on their God-given gifts through the abomination of cloning. The area maintains a top secret status. Zone B, better known as The Acceptables, is where unbeknownst to themselves, residents live as lab rats and are provided for with experimental food and water. Zone C, also known as The Doomed, is heavily populated with most people living underground, a few living in cardboard community areas and all suffering from the toxins that infiltrate water and sewer systems from the daily sprayings and other New World Court law enforcement atrocities. All the world is controlled by the NWC system - businesses, food, agriculture, education, religion, recreation, financial transactions, everything. My name is Angeleigh Aman St. James. I'm 17 years old and I live with my wonderful, sweet, caring and kind-hearted Nana. This past year has been, to say the least, unusual. It took many months before I began to put all the pieces together. What I can tell you is that you must believe. You must have faith to recognize and receive God's blessings. Everyone, EVERYONE, has a special mission appointed to them and be it big or small, it has the same importance to God in His Master plan. Most importantly, you must learn to listen for guidance and instruction from the Spirit that God has placed in each one of us.

This is my story.

CHAPTER ONE

HOPEFUL

*"Therefore, I tell you, whatever you ask for in prayer,
believe that you have received it, and it will be yours."
Mark 11:24*

I LIVE IN HOME region number 22. It is here that Zones B and C
meet, where the elevated trains pass over Front Avenue at the edge
of the Wiskonset River. It is here that mattressed communities
line the underpass and hundreds of people, two-thirds of them
children, reside with a riverside view. I watched intently as the train
I traveled on passed over them. My eyes began to cloud. Many of
the homeless slept below while the river breezes attempted to calm
the 104 degree June heat this early Friday morning. The children
played as children do. They didn't know that their way of life was
anything more than one big camping trip. Well, at least the little
ones didn't. Once these children reached six years of age and were
living on the street, they were really quite grown. This life had a
way of doing that to them, changing their perspective. It had a
way of dismissing the very years of their life that taught them the
importance of stability. It taught them that to feel secure made
them vulnerable, so they distrusted everything and every day they
lived, was without a future to hope for.... no future on earth, no

future eternal. It taught them that they were forgotten. All the people in these communities were forgotten to the world. *But not forgotten to Jesus*, I reminded myself. I surveyed the area once more and saw that man again. This time, dressed in a blue suit and white shirt and tie, he was shaving as if in a hurry to get somewhere. *He must be completing his morning grooming routine, maybe before he would head off to work*, I told myself. Of course, this was just one of the million or so stories I'd made up about my homeless friends. After all, one of them could be my father. Maybe this man who could be my father, had landed a job so he could save some money and afford shelter or at least a new mattress, one that wouldn't fall apart from dry rot or the mold caused by the out-of-doors weather extremes. And maybe one day we would meet and he would at least act like he loved me. My mother, well, I didn't expect that much from her. From what I had been told, she lost the strength to survive out there. But I would keep looking for my mother and father, believing that they were alive until I knew otherwise. With my work at the Community Shelter, I had access to so many of the homeless, and I prayed for the day when my mom or my dad would walk through those doors, asking for something to eat, asking for a place to lay their heads in safe sleep. After all, if they were doing well, they would have gotten in touch long ago, you know, to ask how Nana was and to visit their little girl. I knew they would want to see me. I mean, I never did anything that would make them not want to see me. Had I? How many times had I asked God that question? And God always answered me by directing my thoughts to Nana. No more giving a person could she be. It's true what they say about when God closes one door, He opens another. Because when my parents left, Nana was there. And I believe my grandmom wasn't born here on earth. No, I believe she was a pure angel sent down from heaven to care for me. You see, when they left, I was only a few days old. Nana said I was God's little miracle, being born healthy to both parents addicted to crack-cocaine.

God has something very special planned for you, Angeleigh, echoed Nana's compassionate words, golden words, engraved in my memory. *That's why God spared you the pains of addiction,* she'd say.

I loved listening to the stories Nana would tell me about my mother, how she had been a beautiful, kind, strong and talented young woman. She said she was very artistic and once UNICEF had accepted her paintings to be released as greeting cards, with the proceeds going to raise money to help needy children worldwide. Then one day, Nana said mom just changed. She became angry and dissociated from her friends and family. She threw away all of her paintings, broke up her paint brushes and emptied her paint tubes all over her room. She would sneak out the house and stay out all hours of the night. Seven months later, I was born.

Nana said she met my father for the first time in mom's hospital room. He didn't speak much. Nana said he was trying to be a man but, he hadn't had enough years to grow into one and he was just a confused child himself. Days after they came home from the hospital, my mother left me in Nana's arms and was never seen of or heard of again. Neighbors spoke of times they thought they saw my mother begging on neighborhood street corners. They spoke badly of her, not giving thought to the fact that their words hurt my sweet Nana's heart. Neighbors said my mother had become a member of the invisible community, you know, people who hold out their hands begging for food money, non-existent to passersby. Neighbors said she had become an annoyance, but after all, she was hungry. Nana said the people who really weren't homeless ruined it for those who were, as far as handouts go, that is. No one believed them anymore. It was difficult to give away your hard-earned money to entrepreneurs posing as the destitute and who looked at you as just another rich fool. Of course, things are so different now. Paper money has been replaced with government transaction cards of which the homeless aren't entitled, and without it, they don't have a chance to survive unless they can get in line early at a shelter or mission. Those living in cardboard communities with branded numbers on their faces are issued government leftovers. No telling what the food is made of, but when it makes the people sick, they're escorted by NWC police to unknown locations for unknown purposes.

Well... getting back to my mother, Nana never saw her again - not in the neighborhood, not on the street, not anywhere. Maybe she didn't want to see. Maybe she couldn't look.

I scanned the Cardboard Community #22 one last time, hoping to locate the two people who had given me life. Perhaps the heart that had once beaten so close to mine, that had kept me warm and protected for nine cherished months, would also be searching for me. But no one looked even remotely like the pictures that Nana took of the three of us, the day my parents left me. I will never forget their faces. My mother was such a beautiful woman. Her azure blue eyes, her waist length, silky black hair, her strong and lean athletic body, all too soon began wasting away from the terrible deteriorating effects of the drugs that were consuming her life. Of course, Nana blamed herself. She said she just wasn't in touch with what was going on in the world and she hadn't prepared her daughter to be street smart. Sometimes I'd hear Nana crying uncontrollably in the middle of the night when her guilt overwhelmed her. And my dad, well, Nana didn't have much of a chance to get to know him but, she said she could read behind his tough stare. He seemed streetwise and he acted full of life but, she said he was empty inside. However, he definitely showed an undying love for my mother. He would do anything for her. Nana said that's where their long walk down 'Money, Greed and Lust Avenues' would lead to an eventual deadly end. Nana had her own poetic way with words sometimes. But, to continue my story, though I assumed the drugs consumed them both, I would forever search for my parents. I had studied so many faces that sometimes everyone looked like them. I just couldn't face the fact that they might not be looking for me.

"Next stop, Wiskonset River Drive," announced the computerized train voice. Unlike other areas, Zone B still had what remained of an archaic transportation system, even though, all underground tracks had been cut off and reconstructed into above ground operations. As the doors of the train opened, the heat hit me like a six hundred degree oven. But, this was the last day of school and all I had to do was pick up my belongings from science lab and say goodbye to a few people. That gave me two hours to return home before the twelve noon curfew. You see, no one was allowed on the streets in the B zones between twelve and four p.m., until the aerial vehicles finished their daily cleansing of the neighborhoods, until the caustic spraying was over. The government tried to convince the public that they were decontaminating the atmosphere from all harmful bacteria, to keep us all 'New World healthy', however I had different suspicions.

For my own safety, I needed to keep those suspicions to myself until the right time.

CHAPTER TWO

KINDNESS

"Do not forget to entertain strangers, for by so doing some people have entertained angels without knowing it." Hebrews 13:2

HEAT SLITHERED OVER THE sidewalks lazily like a bad odor. The morning air was thick and hard to breath. Buses were sticky, hot and much too overcrowded to board. So I took the train and after exiting, I decided to walk the four blocks to New World Court High Division 473. Besides, the street vendors were enticing me with their icy treats. They were one of the few normal parts of life left in this community. Most vendors had lost their businesses when they were limited to only three or four business hours per day due to the curfews. Very little self-employment remained in this new world order except for government franchises which were offered to winners through a lottery. I looked down the street and tried to take a deep breath. Despite today's sweltering heat, the sky was an unusual clear blue and reminded me of the seas surrounding the Bahama Islands in old travel logs on the Internet. It was quite a refreshing change from the normal pea green color of the sky by day and the phosphorescent purple tint by night. And I realized that with school almost over for the summer, it was good to be alive and a good day to thank the Lord for all His blessings. I noticed my favorite vending stand open and I decided to stop for something cool and sweet.

"Two iced doughnuts and two cans of apple juice, please."

"Two! Now, I like a hardy eater," said the old man in the booth.

"Oh, it's not all for me," I said. "My grandmom always taught me to share our blessings with others. It's kind of a habit now."

I peered over the counter, into the ice water filled compartment. "Could I have two cans from the bottom, please, if it isn't too much trouble, Sir?"

"No problem," said the old man, "it has to be a hunerd and five out here. Can't wait to go home but, I have to pay ma taxes, ya know. The Mrs., she tells me to get off my duff and go make something of meself." The gentleman laughed showing a mouthful of purple tinted teeth, which wasn't an unusual sight being the result of the contaminated water that so many had to drink when government issued water supplies were scarce. "I'm ninety-two for heaven's sake! But work keeps me young, ya know," the old man laughed heartily as if from deep down in his soul. "That'll be two seventy five, young lady."

I handed over my New World Court Money Transaction card, its motto- 'don't lose it or there'll be repercussions'.

"Ya know, little lady, I remember the good old days of real money. Can't quite get used to this yet." The old man keyed in my identification numbers into his laptop. "If you can't count it at the end of the day, ya feel like you're working for free. And with taxes as high as they are, that's not far from the truth. You know, all I make goes into an account, the government takes theirs and I'm left with what they want to give me. Hmm..." He sat back and with bewilderment, shook his head as he looked up and down the street, "strange... strange world we live in now, youngster. Well, here's your card. You be safe and God bless you child."

I placed one of the juice cans against my face. The ice cold aluminum felt good. I turned the corner to take a shortcut and nearly fell over the feet of my old friend, Lady Maggie.

"Trying to trip me, Miss Maggie?" I said. She let out a big smile.

"Now that's a happy face. What are you doing out in this heat? You should be back at the shelter where it's air conditioned!"

Lady Maggie sat up against the steel mesh fence, wearing her usual wardrobe of everything she owned, the very same as her winter attire. She had to be roasting in all those clothes. I guess the Lord provides a kind of climate control for the homeless. Too many years of living on the street reflected in every wrinkle of her sweet face and emphasized the hard life she'd endured. Her cardboard community number was tattooed across her left cheekbone. Her frail and dirty hands cried out for someone to notice and care.

"Here you go, Maggie," I handed her a doughnut and juice and a tract on hope that I'd made on my home computer. "Now I want you to come by the shelter later. We're having your favorite - macaroni and cheese and ham casserole."

Maggie's eyes sparkled at the thought.

"And I'll save you an extra large piece of Nana's sweet potato pie." No one made sweet potato pie like Nana. No one. It's the stuff dreams were made of.

Maggie smiled and her eyes said yes. In all the years I'd known her, she never uttered a word, but instead used certain hand and facial gestures to communicate with me.

"Great, I'll see you there. Now take this bus voucher. You need to be off the street before twelve noon, remember?"

She nodded her head yes and I patted her hand as I walked away, leaving her with - "I love you, Maggie."

CHAPTER THREE

CONFUSED

"We are hard pressed on every side, but not crushed;
perplexed, but not in despair..."
2 Corinthians 4:8

NWC HIGH DIVISION 473 was quiet, almost eerie. Most students didn't show up on the last day. But then most students didn't feel as close as I did to a teacher like Mrs. Woodrow. Next to my grandmom, Mrs. Woodrow, my homeroom teacher, was like a mother to me. She always made herself available to my needs as well as to all her students. When someone's shoes were worn, she bought them a new pair. When someone didn't have adequate winter clothing, she'd place a surprise coat or boots or mittens in their locker. When I was having difficulty understanding Latin, Mrs. Woodrow made up special conversation tapes for me to practice dialogue. She took her homeless students with their substance abuse problems out of the shelters and into her own home to recover with her love and compassion. She was a good and caring friend after God's own heart. So, you see why I needed to thank her and say good-bye for the summer months.

I walked through the dark, echoing halls to the front door of her home room and peered through the window. There she sat, engrossed in last minute paperwork on her computer. She looked almost angelic with the sunlight filtering through her light reddish hair. A few students sat by the classroom window discussing their summer online projects. I tiptoed up to Mrs. Woodrow and wrapped my arms around her shoulders in a daughter/mother embrace and placed a brightly wrapped gift in front of her.

"Ooh...I love surprises! Now who could this be behind me?"

"Just your biggest admirer," I replied, "I hope you'll like it. I found it in the back room of the shelter where they saved some of the gifts from the old Christian store on Main Street before the government banned them."

Mrs. Woodrow paused for a minute. "I do so miss shopping in Christian stores. I miss the encouragement, the inspiration..." Mrs. Woodrow smiled as she carefully unwrapped the silver paper and opened the gold box that held a delicate Noah's Ark figurine. "This is wonderful, Angeleigh."

"Go ahead, Mrs. Woodrow, wind it up," I said.

She turned the key and the little boat began to rock as if in rough waters while the animals danced to the tune of "Wind Beneath My Wings". Tears welled in her eyes as she watched the musical figurine dance. "I will treasure this forever," she said as she placed it in full view on her desk.

"So, Angeleigh...how will you be spending your summer?"

"Well, of course I'll be at the shelter most of my time," I said with excitement. "I'll be organizing an activities room. We have so many more occupants now than before the street restrictions. There are so many children now, Mrs. Woodrow. I... I just want to give them plenty of fun and inspirational activities to fill their time."

Mrs. Woodrow let out a deep breath. "The children...many lost their parents to the aids plague of 2105...I, uh"...she shook her head as she pondered the awful memory of the millions who were attacked by a new strain of a virus that couldn't be treated. Then she straightened her posture and released her usual dose of compassionate encouragement- "I have a lot of materials at the church that are no longer used, plenty to share - movies, books, games, some posters maybe and a large box of art supplies!"

"That would be great, but you'll get in trouble. You know sharing books is banned. They say they're disease transmitters."

"Yes, that's the same thing they said about libraries and so they shut them down many years back. I never believed libraries were hazardous to your health. The NWC just wanted to control the public's access to an abundance of knowledge. They're not that concerned about people's welfare and I don't think they'll be checking the shelter, Angeleigh. Let this just be our little secret, okay?" she said with raised eyebrows.

"Thank you so much, Mrs. Woodrow. I can pay you of course..."

"You can pay me nothing! We're partners in Christ, remember!" Mrs. Woodrow reached out to hug me.

"I'll miss you over the summer," I said.

"Oh, you'll see plenty of me because I have a lot of resources for your projects. Now you'd better be on your way. It's almost eleven o'clock, only an hour to get home." Mrs. Woodrow motioned to the rest of the lingering students. "You must be on your way now, ladies and gentlemen."

As I turned to leave the classroom, Mrs. Woodrow called to me. "Angeleigh, come by the school next Monday. I'll have some of those donations. Hurry now child, you have some distance to get home."

I smiled in acknowledgement and proceeded to the science lab, but my warmed spirit was quickly chilled by a strange presence in the halls of High Division 473. The locker lined walls, the slate floors, the cathedral high ceilings, though they were definitely inorganic I could feel something ...something alive... something moving around me...watching me... waiting. My surroundings felt dismal, frigid, and lonely. My heels chillingly echoed in the halls as

I ran to remove myself from this frightening eeriness. A sense of cold passed through my body from front to back.

I quickly turned my head to look, though not really wanting to know what might be lurking behind me. A strong whiff of rotten meat permeated the still air and I shook as the smell cut through my sinuses like knife-wielding smelling salts. I felt alone and extremely vulnerable. As I ran to science lab, I began praying from Psalm 46:1, *"God is our refuge and strength, an ever-present help in trouble."*[1]

I flew open the door and as it closed behind me, I supported my quivering frame against the classroom wall and peeked through the steel-mesh window. I prayed that the lights of the lab would deter my evil stalker from following me inside.

No sooner had I felt a sigh of relief that it must all be in my imagination, a hideous, hunched, dark shadow appeared on the other side of the thin window pane. It paused at the door, faced me, looked straight into my eyes with a bone-chilling hypnotic stare, and then quickly disappeared into the dim, yellow lit, darkness of the corridors. I searched for a deep breath and almost choked, my mouth, so dry and parched. I looked around the science lab. No one was paying me any mind, as though this was my own little personal horror show. Five bio heads, as many called the school's science geniuses, sat in one corner of the room, debating and comparing their home lab experiments. Two girls sat up front, combing each other's hair. I took another deep breath, and walked to the far corner of the room to gather myself as well as my science fair project and belongings. As I stood at the window searching for an ounce of normalcy, I noticed three children, no older than nine or ten, conducting business as usual for some despicable neighborhood drug lord.

My fear instantly turned to rage. The New World Court police are there to serve you a summons if you share a book with someone. But babies selling drugs on street corners? That was legal because it could at least rid society of more of the oppressed. Though the NWC patrolled and protected the areas continually, residents of zone B were definitely known to be expendable. After all, we weren't Zone A Biosphere Six material.

"Ang...hey, Ang!" Kyra nudged my shoulder and grimaced at the expression on my face. She began rubbing my shoulder in compassion. "These guys bothering you again?" Kyra asked. "You know you see them every day."

"Hey old friend," I replied. Kyra, my long-time ally since kindergarten knew me well. "I'll never get used to them, maybe it's personal."

"You can't save the world, Angeleigh. For someone who does so much for so many people, you sure stay miserable! When are you going to start feeling good about yourself?" said Kyra looking frustrated. We'd been through this so many times before and she gave me the same lecture every time. *Lighten up*, she'd say, *You of all people know that God wants you happy so you can spread joy when you do His work.* And though her intentions were good, her words couldn't prevent me from going deeper inside myself where a door to deep depression was always left unlocked. *Don't let the devil steal your joy*, she'd always say, *you're one of the good guys! Yeah...one of the good guys*, I'd always reply.

"You know you could have been one of the doomed people." Kyra looked at me with one eyebrow slanted upward. "I hear their skin melts right off them when it rains."

"That's disgusting. I think you're being a bit dramatic."

"Well, they can't be living a good life or they wouldn't be called the doomed people now would they!" Kyra said with more than her normal dose of cynicism.

"All I know is that I feel like ripping up this stupid project." I looked at the title so meticulously positioned across the top of the poster board – Faith vs. Reasoning and Their Effects on the Brain. "I mean, how dumb am I to think that anyone believes in God anymore, Kyra. No one believes in anything anymore! What planet am I from?"

"I don't know, but I think we should see if more of you would like to live on planet earth." Kyra grabbed my arm in her always gentle but assertive way. "Now, come on, you're tired and this is the last day of school" Kyra pushed me out the classroom door. "All I want to do is go someplace COOL," she continued, "because THIS HEAT IS KILLING ME!"

We walked slowly down the sweltering hot streets to the depot and boarded the train that was on standby for its next scheduled run. There were plenty of empty seats which allowed the circulation of the air conditioning to be so much more relieving.

Kyra sat nearest the window and stared, appearing deep in thought. "I'll be going down to visit my cousin in the country," Kyra said and hesitated momentarily. "We'll be down there for two weeks."

"You don't look too happy about it," I commented.

"I don't feel so happy. I mean, my cousin Jamie and I have a lot of fun together and I love to look at the lake and...I..."

Kyra looked like she was about to cry. I grabbed her hand and held it tight.

"It's just that Jamie is sick," Kyra's voice began to weaken. "And they say he won't get better and I'm afraid I'll lose him, Angie."

"They never found out what was wrong with him, I guess."

"The doctors say it's his immune system, it's not what it's supposed to be. He can't keep food down, he has skin rashes...," Kyra's lips were quivering as she held back the tears. "My family is afraid he has the virus. He's declining slowly and if the New World Court finds out..." I put my arms around her shoulders as she quietly let the tears flow. "My aunt cares for him the best she can with non-New World Court doctors to keep his condition private. But I'm really scared, Angie."

The silence was painful. I searched for words to comfort her. "Remember when we were little, Kyra. We all used to sit around and concoct crazy ideas to make candy money. Hmm," I giggled nervously. "Jamie would set up a stand and sell anything his mom had in the refrigerator - lemonade...milk...cake...even cheese slices. He was so comical."

A long silence followed. As the train sped to our destination, I stared at the window and at Kyra's reflection. She was so deep in pain.

"Kyra," I said softly as I patted her hand. "C'mon now. This is our stop."

As the doors of the train opened, I almost fell into a little elderly woman, blocking my exit. She wore a strange black garb that almost completely covered her small frame.

"I'm so sorry ma'am. Excuse me," I said.

The strange little woman was making grumbling sounds, barely audible, "Angel, they wait...they wait for you."

"What did she say, Kyra? She knew my name!" Kyra and I peeked at each other over our sunglasses. Fear grabbed our legs as if childhood monsters under the stairs were holding us back. We tried our best to move and finally our will won over fear and we quickly ran onto the train platform and out the station yelling, "IT'S DEFINITELY ICE CREAM TIME!"

CHAPTER FOUR

DISCOURAGED

"Wait for the Lord; be strong and take heart and wait for the Lord." Psalm 27:14

MY NEIGHBORHOOD WAS LOUD and busy. People stood on every step, most arguing, others laughing. It was summer, but the spirit was far from sunny. I saw a group of my old classmates from junior high quarreling in front of old Mr. Nabor's grocery. There was Caleb, who was very smart, in fact, at the top of his class. He had aspirations to become a mathematics professor. But street drugs kept talking to him and unfortunately, they won the debate. And Jessie, another friend who wanted to go into business, perhaps manage a computer wholesale webstore, was swayed by too many of his friends who said that it was better to do nothing than to give in to the government and run one of their franchised businesses. Such was the story of so many of my old classmates. They woke up each day to no hope. They didn't believe in themselves and they didn't believe they had a future. Worst of all, they didn't believe in God. They lied, they cheated, they robbed. They had no value for life - not theirs, not anyone's. They were always in some kind of trouble. They were often arrested and after being evaluated by the NWC police, all charges would be dropped as if their evil deeds were to be applauded, almost rewarded. They didn't care if they lived to see tomorrow because they had nothing to hope for today. Sometimes I would pass out encouragement tracts to them, but they laughed at me and threw them in the gutters. Sometimes I asked them if they would like to help out down at the shelter, thinking that if they could offer hope to others, maybe they would find some hope for themselves. I know you can't force belief down anyone's throat. It's just that I didn't want them to die without knowing the truth. But they told me to leave them alone. My friends were falling to the wayside and all I could do was watch.

Life had become so negative. People were giving up and giving in to the new world order. With churches forced to close their doors due to NWC mandates, it had become very difficult to spread the Gospel to anyone, let alone reach the masses. Although the government had not yet banned private Bible reading and prayer, people who wanted to have a personal relationship with Christ were afraid to expose their religious beliefs for fear of repercussions from the New World Court. It was so bad that I often wondered if anyone still believed that God would even listen to their prayers. There were just so many lost that needed to be reminded of His eternal love. I felt helpless, but not hopeless. I knew my many prayers for God's children would someday be answered. Yet tears still robbed my eyes of sleep in the late-night hours. As much as my faith taught me the futility of worry, I was human, and often times it possessed me.

My neighborhood alone gave me much to pray for. Once spirit filled churches, were now boarded up sanctuaries of abandoned hopes. Deserted storefronts, overcrowded corners busy with pointless activities, idle teenagers satisfying addictions, the young dying over the wrong color shirt, curtains blowing out the screen-less windows of foreclosed homes, the static sounds of empty TV stations bouncing off the bare walls of love-lost dwellings, and babies crying in need of love, portrayed the dismal atmosphere. But among this chasm of desolation, there stood one refuge of spiritual sustenance. Adorned with bright passion pink and deep lavender-colored flowers in white garden planters, with freshly painted wooden awnings shading a peaceful front porch, one home gave hope to this neighborhood, at least in my eyes. It was my Nana's home. And grandmom's goodness and faith in God prevailed in everything she touched. It was like a breath of cool, fresh air just to envision this sweet dwelling. As Kyra and I lazily walked to the front of my home, we stopped a minute to talk.

"You're a good friend, Kyra. You're always there for me." I grabbed her hand. "And don't worry about your cousin Jamie. Though it might not seem like it, God is in control." I hugged my dear friend. "Now, I have to go see if Nana needs help with the shelter dinners. I'll see you back here in ten minutes for ice cream, okay?" Waving as I ran up my front steps, I yelled back to her, "Ten minutes, Kyra!"

"Well, we've got to hurry, Ang," Kyra reminded me. "I need ice cream and it's only twenty minutes until curfew and I need ICE CREAM!"

Before entering my front door, I let down the clear plastic shield over Nana's ivy cascaded steps to protect her plants from the noon spraying. Between the fragrance of the climbing jasmine and my grandmom's cooking, surely you would think you had died and gone to heaven.

"Hi, Nana! Where are you?" I called as I entered the front screen door. "I'm home!" The house was decorated immaculately with perfectly preserved provincial furniture from the late nineteen hundreds, hanging houseplants of every shade of green imaginable, and fresh greenhouse garden flowers in colorful pottery, all thriving on the love grandmom gave them. It was such a comfortable house. Grandmom brought the beauty of the outside in.

"Nana!" I called as I walked through the narrow hallway leading to the den, then through the dining room and finally to her sweet-smelling shed kitchen.

"Hello, dear. I'm busy making biscuits. The ones in the oven for the shelter are almost done. I'm making a few more for us." Grandmom snickered. "I know how much you love these biscuits. And I just feel like doing a lot of baking today!"

Cooking for the community shelter was Nana's favorite pastime. And it was a pastime definitely appreciated by many. Everyone looked forward to grandmom's evening meals. She didn't cook all the food but one thing was for sure, all her delicacies disappeared before the rest of the donations and she could do more with SR-Six government manufactured nutritionals than anyone, anywhere. Grandmom worked diligently preparing the dough for her rich and buttery sweet biscuits. I watched as her arthritic hands kneaded love into her baked goods. At eighty-two years of age, she was determined to stay active and strong. And though she suffered from the usual pains of old age, she would never show it. She always said it would do no good. She said she was too poor to be sick. I promised God that when I grew up, I would always have enough money to pay for grandmom's medical bills. If there was one person in the world who didn't deserve hurt, it was Nana.

"Made all the favorites today, dear!" said Grandmom with her loving enthusiasm. Across the table lay the most magnificent creations of culinary expertise, a sumptuous display of mouth-watering delicacies. From the rich and creamy casserole of cheddar, ham and noodles, browned to perfection for tang and crunch; to the fresh and still hot, sweet potato pies (you could taste the ever so delicate touch of lemon that enhanced the sweetness of the potatoes). Oh, and at the end of the table sat her twelve egg, marble pound cake awaiting its half inch thick layer of chocolate pecan frosting. Watching grandmom working in the kitchen turned you into a kid in a candy store. You wanted some of everything.

"All this good food and yet behind those big beautiful eyes, I see sorrow, my sweet little Angeleigh," said Grandmom with an open heart yearning to understand.

I never could hide anything from her. My face was always an open book to my emotions. "Nothing new...just all the hopelessness I see out in the world. I just feel so useless Nana. I want to make a difference." I was a bit upset, but I couldn't resist sticking my finger in the thick and gooey chocolate frosting. Out came a big chunk of pecan mixed in the velvety smooth chocolate bliss.

"I think all you need is a big bowl of frosting," replied grandmom with a smile.

"Aw come on, Nana, I'm being depressed here," I said and realizing my words, turned my head to conceal my sheepish grin.

"Listen Angeleigh, God has special plans for you, dear. He will use you to your fullest potential in His good time. You just need to wait on Him."

As usual, grandmom, the ever-present love of my life was right, but my patience left something to be desired.

"You're right, Nana," I heaved a sigh and gave her a big hug. "I'll be alright. I better get some boxes from the store for all this good food before the noon curfew. And I'm going to grab an ice cream bar with Kyra. I'll get you one too. I'll be back." I ran down the hall and out the house, calling back the words that I never failed to say - "I love you, Nana." As the door slammed behind me, I looked down the street and saw Kyra waiting patiently. A gentle breeze was kicking up, fighting off some of the motionless, searing heat. As I walked down the steps and into the street, waving to my good friend, a loud crash came from behind and startled me. People began to run in every direction. Again, I looked for Kyra. She was still standing in the same spot, but her hands were covering her mouth as if she was in shock. Then not a second later, crowds blocked her from my view. Loud sirens alerted the neighborhood that police and emergency medical vehicles were coming closer and closer. The police tried desperately to get to the victim, moving the crowds to the curb. I felt that I was in the way. Though I wanted to help do something, I didn't know how. I asked the people next to me what had happened, but in all the confusion and the noise, no one replied. I could see the ambulance pulling up and the Emergency Medical Technicians putting a body on the stretcher. From where I stood, I just couldn't discern who the victim was. I was relieved to see Kyra again. It looked as though she was near the door to the ambulance, but then once again she disappeared. More and more people were pushing into the scene of the accident, separating us and I decided it was best for me to go home and try to call Kyra later. Maybe she would know who had been hurt. In all the chaos, I was beginning to get so confused that my head began to spin, my vision blurred. And then just like in the school corridors, a dark shadow began circling around me, doing its best to unnerve me. As it passed before me, it paused momentarily as it did before, and then quickly disappeared into the crowds. I had to go home. I had this tremendous compulsion just to go home. I pushed my way through the people and began running. It was as if something ungodly was attacking my spirit and I needed to talk to my grandmom. I flew up my front steps, three at a time, so fast that my shoes fell off and almost caused me to fall through the front screen door.

CHAPTER FIVE

VISION

"He stretches out the heavens like a tent and lays the beams of His upper chambers on their waters. He makes the clouds His chariot and rides on the wings of the wind." Psalm 104:2-3

"Nana!" I screamed as I ran to the shed kitchen. Nana's bakeware and preparations lay across the table, the oven still on. Everything was the same as when I'd left, except Nana wasn't there. I felt sick inside. It didn't make any sense. Nothing was making any sense. I started turning in circles looking for her. She had to be alright. I knew she couldn't have passed me on my way out to meet Kyra. *I'm being ridiculous,* I said to myself. *Grandmom has to be alright. She couldn't have been the one in the accident. Grandmom has probably just gone out to see what had happened, worried about me no doubt and she'll walk in the front door any minute now. She's alright.* I kept telling myself, *she has to be alright.* I ran up to the second floor and looked out Nana's front bedroom window to get a better view. The street was carpeted with people. "I have to stop worrying or what good is my faith!" I said loudly. "I'm not supposed to worry. All things work according to His purpose." But trying to convince myself wasn't working very well. As I stood in grandmom's room, I could smell her scent. She always smelled of fresh baked goods and sweet handmade lilac perfume. I looked around her room, searching for anything that would give me a clue of her whereabouts. Everything was in its place and reminded me of her joyful and orderly presence. I picked up a small flower pot of African Violets in full bloom and thought of the care grandmom gave her plants. *She's alright,* I told myself. But I couldn't stop from shaking. Then the three warning signals for noon curfew began to sound. They were sharp and shrill, ugly sounds, reminding me of the New World Court system. I needed to think. I needed to pray. *I'll go to my special spot in the backyard,* I told myself. On my way downstairs I checked every room hoping that grandmom was in one of them. Maybe she had collapsed or something and she couldn't call to me. But there was no trace of her. I looked out the kitchen window at the yard. No one could actually see me out there. And they wouldn't begin spraying our area for another thirty minutes. *I'll just stay out there a few minutes,* I told myself. I sneaked out, all the while looking around to make sure no one saw me. The grass felt good under my toes. I plopped down on my favorite secluded spot surrounded by thick lilac bushes near the back picket fence. Somehow the spraying never bothered the grass or the bushes. This was my haven from reality. I used to lie here for hours in the afternoons before the spraying restrictions began. The clouds told me stories. I always wondered what it must look like from up there, perhaps from an airplane. Now that inter-zone travel was forbidden, plane trips were a long forgotten pleasure. I wondered if from up there you could make some sense of this life, you know, get a better perspective. But my thoughts quickly turned to grandmom. It wasn't like her to just run off without leaving a note or something. I quickly sat up and closed my eyes. *Regroup Angeleigh,* I told myself. The bright warm sunlight pen-etrated my eyelids, creating a sort of lightshow of sparks dancing in rhythmic formations. They danced playfully, rays chasing after each other, criss-crossing and forming intersecting lines like rungs on a ladder. *This is beautiful,* I thought, but I needed to get up and find grandmom. I fought to keep my eyes closed to enjoy this fantasy, but I couldn't waste any more time. I tried to tear myself away, but the fantasy wouldn't tear away from me. I blinked to test my eyes true perception, but the fantasy was my reality... a reality of a ladder of lights that began on the ground, and extended into the clouds above through the blue sea of hazy air blanketing this hot earth this strange summer day.

I sat mesmerized at this celestial vision that held me captive. As I slowly raised myself up off the ground, I found myself reaching for the rungs of this visionary ladder, as if I could attempt to climb, as if I would attempt to climb! I touched the delicate lights and found it curious that they were neither hot nor cold nor liquid nor tangible in any conceivable way. I needed to find Nana but my spirit told me to climb. For some reason, not knowing where this vision would lead me, didn't the least bit frighten me. I tested the first step and it surprisingly held my weight. Then one step after another, I proceeded higher and higher, all the while watching as the treetops became a canvas on which I could paint my dreams of a better world. I looked down at my feet and I wondered what on earth was holding me up. But that was probably just it, nothing on earth was holding me up. This was something else, something other realm-like. With only a small distance to go, I stopped to look down to the world for Nana one more time. All I could see was confusion in the streets. The last few steps led me onto the surface of the clouds. I was about to know what it was like to step out onto a cloud! A cloud? *I'd come this far,* I thought, *no point in getting skeptical now.* My faith told me that God always directs my paths even in strange circumstances. And this could definitely be considered a strange circumstance. So I moved with sure footing. I looked to my right and I looked to my left. I looked behind me and I looked ahead of me.

This was the place of my daydreams. This was the haven I'd longed to visit since early childhood, since the first day that I lay face up on my cool patch of grass. Before me lay an unbelievable landscape of sparkling snow and ice mountains glistening in the sunlight like precious jewels in the hands of God. Gentle waterfalls trickled into tranquil pond waters. Other light staircases appearing as strands of sparkling diamonds, cascaded into sunlit rooms in the distance. This crystalline iced paradise appeared to go on forever and I could feel an overwhelming presence of compassion and love, a beautiful dichotomy of warmth in a sea of snow and ice. In a very odd way I felt as if I belonged here. Welcoming me was a slowly approaching band of strange yet amiable-looking inhabitants of this cloud. They were tall, shimmering creatures with a silk-like translucence, and a rippling and undulating glow that formed the appearance of a flowing robe around them. Deep within their center shone a bright inner light that changed colors with their movement. One of these beautiful creatures stepped forth and spoke in a slow and gentle, sweet motherly tone from a voice deep inside her, as she had no lips with which to speak.

CHAPTER SIX

REVELATION

" 'No eye has seen, no ear has heard, no mind has conceived what God has prepared for those who love Him'- but God has revealed it to us by His Spirit." 1 *Corinthians 2: 9, 10*

"HELLO, ANGELEIGH, MY NAME is Peace. We welcome you and are very pleased that you have finally arrived."

I wondered why this heavenly being said, 'finally.'

Peace continued. "You are very special to us. Come... we will sit and relax and talk." Peace offered the tip of her wing on which to lay my hand. This lifted me and I, along with the other inhabitants in my welcome party hovered along the surface of the cloud, passing through gardens of shimmering ice statues and powdery snow structures and along fountains of the clearest ice water. Perched on a wisp of fine stratus clouds was an assemblage of white doves, peacefully chirping in song. We proceeded to a snowy white valley in which sat an immense, transparent sanctuary of sort that blended almost invisibly into the surrounding environment. As Peace guided me to a place to sit near a tranquil, trickling brook, I touched the snowy powder beneath my feet and found it to be strangely warm to the touch.

"Ma'am, please tell me, if my Nana is okay? And Kyra?"

"Yes, my dear Angeleigh, they are both well. They were not involved in the accident that you observed."

Another inhabitant moved forward and spoke. "I am known as Love and you have entered what we call the 'Holy Sanctuary of Purity, In Righteousness, In Truth'. It is here you can hear our thoughts as well as we can hear yours. We are so very pleased that you have finally accepted our invitation to enter the portal and visit us."

This must be the one in charge, I thought. *Love appeared stronger, taller. But I didn't understand why they kept saying that I 'finally' arrived and I wondered if the staircase had always been there, inviting me to climb?*

Love continued. "You were not mentally prepared to visit us until now, however your heart was always ready. And yes, the stairway has always been there for you. The chosen cannot see until their heart accepts what gifts they've been given."

"Excuse me for asking, ma'am, but how..."

"We relate by mental transference and we move by the guided direction of the most Holy One. All of us live in a fluid environment. Those who understand don't fight the flow of things. We accept that which is not visible to the eyes but only apparent to the spirit. Mankind, however, fights the natural and seeks the unnatural – a very unhealthy habit that causes his sickness and despair."

"Let me introduce to you our Sanctuary administrators. This is Gentleness." She was of a smaller structure than the rest and her face showed complete tenderness. As she nodded in acknowledgement, her wing rose up to her forehead and fluttered down in recognition. Love introduced each of the inhabitants and each waved their wing in affirmation. "Next we have Patience and Joy, Faithfulness, Kindness, Goodness and Self-Control. Now I will allow Faithfulness to explain to you our need for your help."

"Dear Angeleigh...we have observed you for many years and in that you have displayed such a constant of loving kindness for others in your young life, we feel your assistance would be given with the purest effort."

Faithfulness paused as she looked down in despair. "Your world has almost lost all compassion for each other and is close to destroying any means of understanding and accepting the blessings from our Father in Heaven. The Most Holy One hasn't given up on His children but mankind has almost completely given up on God. There are many changes on earth that you are not yet aware of, terrible ungodly changes. Soon mankind won't remember how to find their connection to the Lord Most High."

Kindness continued. "You must spread the message, my dear Angeleigh. You must enlighten them that they can't receive God's blessings if they don't believe in the love He has for them. It is your mission to tell them that they must believe and communicate with The Most Holy One to beg forgiveness for their sins and accept their blessings to continue the work He's set aside for each one of them. They must embrace the Light of the world for He is their only means of salvation. They must listen to the Spirit within them who will guide them and intercess their prayers. His plan must be fulfilled. The deception must be stopped."

"Begging your pardon, ma'am," I interrupted. "I don't understand why God would need our help to fulfill His plans."

Goodness intervened. "No, God does not require your assistance, but the Lord Most High created the family and as a true Father, He wants His children to be a part of His plan."

Goodness looked up to the heavens as she continued. "You see my dear Angeleigh, when we seek His Kingdom, when we believe that Jesus the Christ is the Son of God and came to earth in the image of man to be the sacrificial Lamb for our sins, then we become a part of God's royal family. And we all have been given work to do for His Kingdom."

Joy spoke. "Your father and mother will assist your mission. First you must find them through our direction."

Self-Control spoke. "As you know, in the most recent years, the evil ones have removed the right for prayer in public places. They have removed the acknowledgement of God from the political doctrines that societies were founded upon. Mankind has lost their direction and they are leaving themselves open for attack. They have relinquished their armor in exchange for lust and greed and as a result of their rejections they are closing the connection that leads to eternal life because of their ignorance of eternal damnation."

Patience spoke. "Very long ago, people lived spiritually. They depended on God for all their needs, and they were assisted by the strength, love and unity of the family that they were blessed with. Those bonds of love, trust and respect were handed down from generation to generation and with the fear of the Almighty, God's children remained faithful and persevered. However as you know from your studies Angeleigh, the Bible tells us that in the end times, *'People will be lovers of themselves, lovers of money, boastful, proud, abusive, disobedient to their parents, ungrateful, unholy, without love, unforgiving, slanderous, without self-control, brutal, not lovers of the good, treacherous, rash, conceited, lovers of pleasure rather than lovers of God – having a form of godliness but denying its power.'* "[2]

"Yes," I replied. "The Bible says *'Have nothing to do with them,'* [2] that they will prey on the weak, that they will never acknowledge the truth... Second Timothy, chapter 3, verses two through five."

"Yes, Angeleigh, you know the Word of God well." Faithfulness placed her wing on my shoulder.

"A short time ago, in spiritual years that is," continued Goodness, "the earth's people entered this very self-centered period. When one only thinks of themselves, they live a very lonely existence. They believe they alone are in charge. They live denying their blessings which are to be shared. They live denying their Father in Heaven who is to be praised." Sorrow covered the face of Goodness like a shroud.

Gentleness continued. "Many don't believe that God exists, so they have no hope. Many don't believe in Heaven or Hell, so they have no conscience." Gentleness backed away and allowed Love to speak.

"We will be with you always. We will speak in Spirit. There are others on earth who are messengers as you are and they will be of great help to you. They will be told when to cross your path as you will be told the same. You must learn to listen Angeleigh, listen to your Spirit. We will be in touch. Now however, you must go. Curfew is over and your grandmother calls for you." All the inhabitants lifted me with their wings and carried me to the clouds edge at my initial arrival point.

"And remember, Angeleigh," Faith said, "Don't be afraid, just believe." [3]

I looked down the light staircase at the world below. There was so much chaos down there. It was so peaceful here. The earth was full of deception. There was so much truth here. It was dark and destructive there and I didn't want to return. It was refreshing here and I didn't want to leave. But I had to. I couldn't leave Nana by herself. And now I had a very important mission. I'd been chosen and I had to carry this through. I looked back at Peace and her accompanying spirits as they retreated, disappearing into the pure mist and gesturing to me a blessed journey. I descended back to, by contrast, hell. As I reached the ground I could hear Nana calling me. I turned slowly and saw the staircase dissipating quickly. Not even the path to truth could exist long on this earth.

"I'm over here, Nana. I'm coming."

"Well, it's time for dinner, dear. I need you to take this food to the shelter. Where were you? I've been very worried!"

It was so good to hear Nana's voice.

CHAPTER SEVEN

CALLING

"Be joyful in hope, patient in affliction, faithful in prayer." Romans 12:12

THE PEOPLE OF THE doomed community called it their heartbeat. A multitude of monitors surveyed every entrance as well as a select assortment of street corners that led to this underground extremist network. Two hundred and twenty-five disposed-of citizens dedicated their lives here. They were some of the most skilled in electronic technology. They were immensely strong people, both in mind and in spirit. They had survived the most horrendous psycho-extermination trials of the early 2060's, when the earth's poorest and broken down souls were faced with the ultimate test of their allegiance to what the New World Court deemed wrong. They were the revolutionaries, the radicals. They were the handicapped of this new world, the sick in body but mighty in Spirit. They were the advocates of truth. Jesus was their Lord and Savior and no government could tell them otherwise. They couldn't be brainwashed according to the New World Court doctrine, so they were left to die as 'the Doomed.' And now they were involved in one of the most important and dangerous of secret operations. Here, busy computers and other tech devices maintained a steady hum of service, but all eyes and ears were directed to the eloquent and steadfast man in the center of the room.

"People, we are at a very critical stage in our project." Well over six feet, the man at center stage stood slightly bent as if the weight of his work lay heavily on his shoulders. Though his complexion was grey from living in the depths of the tunnels, his body remained strong from the intense hours of weight-training workouts that he said stabilized his mind. His hair, long and wavy, was pulled back in a tight ponytail, which brought attention to his passionate eyes that were ignited by the warmth of his enthusiasm and his earnest desire to follow God's will.

"The nature of the New World Court is to take control of our families, people!"

"That's right! Yes!" yelled the crowd.

"They don't want us to look to our Lord and Savior, Jesus Christ for guidance!"

"Preach on Reverend!"

"They don't want unity among the citizens of this lost planet!"

"No, they don't!" shouted the crowd.

"They took away our rights for public prayer. They've separated our families!"

"Oh Lord!" they cried.

"They monitor our daily activities and subject us to lethal viruses. And they control us through our health by playing with the very substance that allows our bodies to keep on functioning – WATER!"

"God be with us," they shouted.

"What can we do, you ask?"

"Yes, preacher."

"We have to expose them for who they are!"

"Right on!" yelled the crowd as they clapped fervently.

"We have to expose the proliferation of the virus!"

"Speak on, brother."

"We have to take back our families and we have to take back the blessings of this earth that God gave us!"

"Hallelujah!" cheered the overwhelmed crowd.

At the entry ways to the room, dark shadows pushed back from the perimeter of Mission City, dissipating into the cold depths of the tunnels, as people joined hands in the singing of "Precious Lord".

"Okay, people, are you ready, willing and able to take on our enemies?"

"Yes, Reverend!"

"Tomorrow at midnight our mission will begin. Thank you, my brothers and sisters. Thank you, family."

The crowd reveled in abundant joy, hugging each other for successfully completing months of tiresome preparation work. Tears flowed down the many smiling faces.

"And as God is our Father in Heaven, we will not be defeated!" said the man known as Michael T, as he made his way back to his office, shaking outreached hands along the way. He personally was responsible for rescuing all one hundred and seventy-five of his family members from extermination and assisted in bringing thousands more to a safe haven. He couldn't allow them to risk their lives now. His plan was solid and he had the best Commander in Chief, the Lord Jesus Himself, guiding his every move. His faith was strong. But throughout history, even the strongest men of faith had their doubts at some time in their walk with God. And though he didn't question God, at times he did question whether he understood what God was telling him to do. He entered his office, quietly closing the door behind him and folded his hands in prayer.

CHAPTER EIGHT

FAITH

"Now faith is being sure of what we hope for and certain of what we do not see." Hebrews 11:1

I WANTED TO SHARE my experience with Nana. I wanted to tell her about the beauty that could be entered through a portal not fifteen feet from our back door. I always told Nana everything. But this...this, I needed to think through first. *Why wouldn't she believe me,* I thought to myself, *she was the most spiritual person I knew.* But this seemed so personal, like your deepest, most secret prayers. Still I started to explain, because I had worried her when she couldn't find me, and her trust meant everything to me. But all that came from my lips was, "I was strange...the clouds, they live there..."

"What did you say, dear?" asked grandmom perplexed.

"I don't know Nana, maybe I need to gather my thoughts. I'm sorry I worried you so." I didn't want to lie to her.

"I was back behind the bushes, deep in thought," I blurted out.

Grandma hugged me. "It's okay dear, you're safe now. But how did you manage to avoid the spraying out there?"

"I covered myself with...um...it's just that after the accident, I couldn't find you, and I..."

"Accident you say, dear?" Nana looked stunned. "What accident, sweetheart?"

"Down the street...someone was hit...and there was an ambulance..." Now I was really stuttering in my confusion.

Nana pulled me close to her. "Calm yourself, dear. You look like you've seen a ghost. Why don't you go get cleaned up for dinner. Maybe you need something to eat."

"Maybe so, Nana," I mumbled as I walked up the stairs to my bedroom. I felt blessed for being appointed to this mission, but you have to admit this was a very difficult experience to comprehend. I needed a moment of quiet, and my room would give me that quiet. Or so I thought. Just as I was going to plop down on my bed, I heard a strange groaning noise that seemed to be coming from the corner of the closet near the window. I almost didn't want to look. But really, what else could possibly shock me. I took a deep breath and risking whatever sanity I had left, I grabbed the knob to my closet door and quickly pulled it open. My stuffed rabbit, whom I so fondly called 'Honey Bunny' fell on my head and nearly stopped my heart. Honey Bunny, now faded from years of laundering, had belonged to my mom and remained my silent friend since I was two. It was sort of my connection to her. The moaning continued however, and now it seemed to be coming from outside. I ran to Nana's room to get a better view of the front of the house and there on the sidewalk lay an elderly woman. So, I ran down the stairs and out the front door to see what I could do to help.

"Ma'am, are you alright? Ma'am!" I asked nervously, kneeling down beside her. A very frail woman dressed in clothes dated before the millennium, lay in a fetal position, struggling to catch her breath.

"Thirty," the old woman muttered.

"What? Thirty?" I asked, straining to decipher her words. "Are you alright, Ma'am?"

"Thirtieth," the old woman said irritably.

"Ma'am, please don't talk...and don't move. I'll call for a doctor."

As I began to get up, the old woman grabbed me by my collar and pulled me close to her, whispering, "You...you...must...go...t o...Thirtieth...Street...Mission ...your father, child....your father." The old woman laid her head back down on the ground, breathing with much labor.

"You just rest, I'll get help." My feet barely touched the steps as I ran into the house to call for an ambulance. My hands were shaking so hard that I dropped the phone and startled Nana.

"What on earth is wrong now, Angeleigh?" asked grandmom in a very high pitched tone.

"Nana...there's a," I said, gasping for air, "there's a lady..." I picked up the phone and started dialing 911, "a lady on the pavement out front," I continued, "she's hurt!"

Nana ran to the door and searched the outside of the house, returning quite puzzled. "Dear, there's no one out there."

"Of course there is, Nana, she's lying..." I dropped the phone and ran out the door to look for myself. "She's lying on...on the..." The elderly woman was gone. I ran down to the corner and looked both ways. I ran to the other corner and looked down that street. *She couldn't have gotten away that fast,* I thought, *even if she wasn't hurt. Even if she wasn't elderly, she couldn't have disappeared that quickly.* I walked back into the house to face my very concerned grandmother over my strange actions. "She was there, Nana, and she kept repeating the word, 'thirtieth'. I have to go out for a while."

"Angeleigh, I'm beginning to worry about you."

"Don't worry, really. I'll be back as soon as I can." I kissed her on the cheek and ran out the door.

"But your dinner, dear. And it's already beginning to get dark outside."

"I love you. Nana." *I have to get to Thirtieth Street Mission,* I thought as I headed for the train depot. *My father might be there.*

CHAPTER NINE

STEADFAST

"You will be secure, because there is hope; you will look about you and take your rest in safety." Job 11:18

I HAD NEVER TRAVELED to the other side of town before. As I descended the stairway from the elevated trains, I looked at the cold darkness of the streets before me.

I must be crazy following the directions of a disappearing old woman, I told myself. *But then she might be one of the messengers that the cloud spirits spoke of.*

One single street lamp illuminated the narrow block of Thirtieth Street, that and the full moon in the pitch black of the night sky. The moon looked particularly ominous and its exceptional brightness caught my attention. I stood mesmerized at the lunar spotlight as clouds whisked past it, encircled it, whirling and whirling before the moon, twisting and twirling until they gradually gave way to the shape of a cross. It was nothing I'd ever seen before. It gave me comfort. It acknowledged the presence of my spirit chaperones and that they were giving me a sign that I shouldn't fear my journey. I looked around, before me and behind me. I could see no signs of life, but I could hear faint distant voices somewhere in the darkness. I felt eyes staring at me from the bleak doorways of this burial ground of abandoned buildings. The echo of my footsteps bounced against the empty brick warehouse walls and was making me a bit paranoid. I turned completely in a circle as I proceeded. Out of the corner of my eye, I caught the glimpse of a dark shadow slithering in through the cracked window of an old Ma and Pa restaurant, circa late nineteen hundreds. Though needless to say, they were trying their best to unnerve me, to make me head back home and forget my assignment. I picked up my pace from a quick nervous strut to a swift sprint, so swift that I barely touched the ground. I ran and I ran, no longer looking back. For two more city blocks, I ran until my sprints turned into leaps.

And then I looked up and there it was, not twenty feet before me, a brightly lit neon sign in the shape of a cross, much like the beautiful vision in the sky outside the subway stop. Below the neon cross read the words – *"Come to Me, all you who are weary and burdened, and I will give you rest."* Matthew 11:28 [4] -30th Street Mission Welcomes You. I ran up the thirty or so steep steps and knocked furiously at the Mission door. It creaked open by itself and I stepped inside to discover an antiquated but nevertheless, cheerfully decorated foyer where an elderly guard sat sound asleep in an old broken down, upholstered chair next to a radiator. Although the notion that he was dead did cross my mind considering the nature of my day, I dismissed the thought. Amidst the aged and yellowed, spider web laced walls, were old and cracked glass framed photographs, which I assumed were of former residents. I studied them, searching for my father and for the disappearing little elderly woman.

"May I help you, young lady?" I was startled by a grey haired man looking to be near ninety years old who approached me from behind. "Is there someone you're looking for?" he said very abruptly.

"Well Sir, yes Sir...I was wondering...um...is there a woman here?" I was still quite out of breath at this point from running. "I'm looking for an elderly woman in her late seventies, I guess. She's frail and she wears a brown crocheted sweater and a bright blue hat with flowers on top. And she uses a cane. Sir, does she live here?"

The man appeared very annoyed with my questions. "Actually young lady, there's no one here over sixty right now and they're all men. Now if there's nothing else, you should be leaving."

"Look Sir, I'm not trying to cause any trouble here, but..."

"I think it's time you leave now." The man grabbed my arm and began escorting me to the door.

"It's just that I found this lady collapsed on the pavement outside my grandmother's bedroom window and she mentioned this mission and my father and then she disappeared."

"I'm sorry, I can't help you." The man opened the door and very impolitely pushed me out.

"Can I just please speak to the person in charge?" I pleaded.

"That would be me," he said and at that he slammed and locked the door.

As I stood on the landing in total disbelief of this man's rudeness, I prayed for guidance for my next step. I thought I was doing what I had been told to do. All the signs pointed to this place on my journey. But now what? I knew that following the Lord isn't always easy, but I'd come so far for virtually no information and I didn't want to leave empty handed. Just then the door opened. It was the old man who had been on guard.

"Young lady, I overheard your conversation with Mr. Greeley. I know I looked asleep. I find out things that I shouldn't that way." He looked a little guilty. "Please excuse his attitude. And please come back in. Old Mr. Greeley, well... he's gone downstairs for a while, so we can talk. Now, just what did this little lady tell you?" The polite gentleman motioned for me to enter and have a seat in his favored, well-worn chair. "I'm Holbert by the way."

"Thank you so much, I'm Angeleigh. Well, she mentioned this place and she mentioned my father. Do you know this lady, sir?"

Holbert pulled up a chair and sat next to me, leaning in to whisper. "Do you believe in the spiritual, child?"

"If you mean do I believe in God, yes Sir, I do."

"Well from your description, it sounds like Mrs. Maple. It's been said that many have seen her here, in the spirit that is. She died a little over ten years back. Before that she was a resident for a good twenty years. Did a lot of the cooking and the cleaning in exchange for room and board."

"So, what has that got to do with my Dad? His name is Michael Thriambeuo."

"Michael T! Michael is your father?" said the old man.

"Sir, you know him?"

"Michael is my son, child." A glow came over the old man's face at the mention of his much loved son.

I was in awe of the situation. So many years of looking for my family and I was sitting this close to the man who had raised my father. My eyes welled with tears and I held out my arms. "Grandfather!" I cried.

My grandfather embraced me with the warmth and compassion that I'd dreamed of for so long. My prayers to know my family were at last becoming a reality. I stepped back to observe the resemblance to the photograph I'd kept of my father. Though my grandfather was so much thinner with age, I could see the similarity in facial structure. Most of all, I could see my father in his eyes. I always noticed the eyes.

"Grandfather," I hesitated for a moment to ask my most anticipated question, fearing the worst answer, "is my father alive?"

"Well, yes child, as far as I know." My grandfather again pulled me close to whisper. "You see, your father went underground years ago."

"He's one of the doomed?"

"Your father is a very important man and I can't talk too much about what he does, at least not here. Let's just say, he was always an activist doing his best to help people and keep families together as God ordained him to do. It became his life's work."

"I thought he was a drug dealer, Grandpa."

"That's what he wanted everyone, especially the government, to believe, to protect his cover. Then he met Elizabeth, your mother. He was much older than her. She was a very sweet girl, but very naive." Grandpa looked to the ground, as if searching for the right words. "Some problems arose that needed to be taken care of. Oh, how they were in love," grandpa grinned from ear to ear. "Not long after they met, Elizabeth became pregnant with you and then, well, your father had to go into hiding and he took your mother with him. I have a picture of the two of them." Grandpa pulled out a warped and flattened leather wallet, the kind people used back when things were bought with paper currency. He very carefully pulled out a photograph of mom and dad.

"You see," grandpa pointed to his daughter-in-law and passed me the yellowed photo. "Your mom is about eight months pregnant here, and your dad, well, you can see much concern in his face. He was always very afraid for her safety. The thing is, your dad had many associates in high New World Court positions, who were really for the cause, for the good fight, to take down this New World Order. They would leak information to him. The NWC suspected he was being informed, but they didn't know by whom. Your mom and dad just weren't safe on the streets. It hurt them terribly that they had to leave you with your grandmother, for safety sake."

"Did Nana know about all this?" I questioned.

"No...no, not at all. That would have jeopardized you and your grandmother."

"So, my parents really do love me?"

"More than you can imagine, child. Enough to give up their sweet, dear little baby, probably never to see again, so she could live in safe keeping with her loving grandmother."

"I thought they hated me all these years, Grandpa. I feel so bad."

"You had no way of knowing, Angeleigh. They rather you hate them than to live in danger."

"Grandfather, where can I find my father?"

"Oh child," grandpa said with caution, "it's very dangerous up there. It's another world you know nothing about."

"But I've got to find my mother and father."

Grandpa took a deep and troubled sigh. "Your mother Elizabeth, she's not underground anymore. They took her, the New World Court police, that is. They took her years ago, brought her up to Biosphere Six up in the hill country. Elizabeth was very gifted and they wanted her for procreation studies. It nearly killed your father when it happened. He didn't want to live without her. Then he realized he had a greater purpose and in fulfilling that purpose, he might be able to rescue your mom along with many others."

"I'll go there, Grandfather. It's along the river, right?"

"Child, security around the biospheres is impenetrable. You best stay out of this, Angeleigh."

"I can't, grandpa. I have to do this. I have to find them. It's a spiritual thing."

Grandpa paused and let out a heavy sigh. "Well, I see you are your father's daughter and leadership is in your blood, child." Grandpa snickered and tried to change the subject. "Did you know Thriambeuo means to lead triumphantly? I was so proud of your father when he decided to follow God's lead." Grandpa smiled and shrugged his shoulders. "Look, I know there's not much I can say to you that will make you change your mind. Tell you what, you come back to see me tomorrow afternoon about two o'clock. We'll take a walk at lunchtime and I'll tell you what you need to know." Grandpa hugged me and kissed my forehead. "God be with you child. You best be on your way now. This neighborhood isn't safe you know, especially after dark."

"Okay grandpa, but just one more thing. What does Mrs. Maple have to do with all this?"

"Well, she knew your dad, brought him here to the mission when he was having some trouble in the street with the new government. He could hide out safely here. In fact, that's how I got this job. After I retired, my life savings didn't last long, wasn't enough to live on. Your dad told me the mission house was looking for a guard. I get room and board in exchange for guard service. So, seems like Mrs. Maple led you to me. Seems like you have plenty of help with the spiritual end of things, child."

I nodded. "I realized that today." Amidst all the danger I seemed to be facing, God's prevailing guidance made me smile. I looked up into the time-worn and loving face of my grandpa and gave him a heartfelt hug goodbye. "I love you, Grandpa and I'll be back to see you tomorrow."

As I waved goodbye, grandpa motioned for me to come back a moment and whispered in my ear. "Everybody but the biospheres are eventually doomed, Angeleigh. We get water rations and medical care, but we're all just lab rats in one way or another. They conquer by separating our families. They conquer by telling us not to pray. Remember, the opposite of faith is fear. And they rely on fear and loneliness to cause people to submit to them. This is what your father is fighting for - to restore faith in mankind, to restore the family as God intended."

"None of this is fair, Grandpa."

"Nothing in life is fair or certain, except God, child. Stay close to Him in all you do."

With that, I ran down the dark and forbidding, deserted streets of this neighborhood, never looking back, thanking God for the opportunity to be an Ambassador for Him, to do the work He so graciously and mercifully called me to do, and thanking Him for bringing me to my grandfather.

CHAPTER TEN

ASSURED

"In God I trust; I will not be afraid. What can man do to me?" Psalm 56:11

I ARRIVED NOT A second too soon. The train pulled into the station at the exact moment that I reached the top of the boarding platform. It was a welcome relief to be leaving this very unsettling part of the city. I boarded the train and leaned against the partition near the door in an effort to compose myself. I glanced at the passengers. Their heads were bowed, appearing to be in silent sleep from their tiring day's work. But there was one man, who sat near the end of the train car, glaring at me with an unremitting gaze. His eyes made me tremble. They were like knives cutting through my flesh, creating an entrance for an entity to invade and shake me from the inside out. I tried looking the other way, but nervously I kept glancing back in his direction. I fumbled in my pockets, really making it obvious how uncomfortable I was. I broke out in a cold sweat. *It must just be my paranoia*, I told myself. I looked up and thought of positive things like being home with grandmom, sitting on the porch, sipping a cool glass of lemonade and enjoying a big slice of her creamy coconut pie. My imagination almost let me feel the cool night breezes coming in from the park. And I thought about the many good things that had happened to me today. I had found out that my parents loved me and I would soon meet them. I had a new grandfather in my life and most of all, God would always be there to protect me. All I had to do was listen and follow Him. And I needed to think of good things. *"Whatever is true, whatever is noble, whatever is right, whatever is pure, whatever is lovely, whatever is admirable-if anything is excellent or praiseworthy-think about such things,"* [5] I told myself. Now if I could just get past this man staring at me, I could relax and enjoy my blessings. *Why do things always get in the way of that?* I wondered, shaking my head. But these cold dark eyes penetrating my thoughts, seemingly knowing my fears, were really getting on my nerves. *Please Lord, keep me safe in your care,* I kept repeating quietly under my breath, comforting my restless heart. I looked out the window, searching for the sign of the cross. It wasn't there anymore, though it remained vivid in my mind. I planned my next move. When I get to my stop and if he follows me, I'll find a station attendant who can call the police. There's no doubt I could identify him. I would remember his face. I would remember his long black mustache that outlined his deceitful smile. I would remember the heavy silver earring in his left ear. I would remember his black clothes, his weather-beaten, black leather jacket. But most of all, I would remember his eyes, his empty, soul-less eyes.

The doors of the train opened and I could feel his stare following me. I walked quickly, focusing only on my destination. Then a loud noise sounding like a gunshot turned my fear into mortal terror.

"I'm going to kill someone tonight," announced a disturbed voice.

Another shot fired. My heart was pounding so hard that my shirt pulsated as if it had a life of its own. I had to know if there was a bullet in the chamber of this transgressor's gun for me or was it just fear making still another attempt to stop me from my mission.

I took a deep breath. The air on the station platform was thick with that familiar dark, pungent mist. Black shadows encircled me, but they kept their distance this time. In what felt like eternity, I awkwardly turned to face what I thought could possibly be my dying moment. The man from the train, the man with the beaten down leather jacket, the man with the soul-less eyes, was waving a New World Court issued, high-powered, extermination weapon.

Police stormed the train station platform. "It's another defector from Bio Six," yelled an officer. With weapons aimed to exterminate, they allowed him one more minute of life as if they were ordered to support his last proclamation.

"I'm going to kill someone," he screamed over and over again, turning his body wildly in all directions until he turned to face me, pointing his gun, staring with his cold, empty, heartless eyes and said, "And that someone is you."

Shots rang and the attacker was diminished to dust.

CHAPTER ELEVEN

SAFEGUARD

"Are not all angels ministering spirits sent to serve those who will inherit salvation?"
Hebrews 1:14

Tommy Watchthee sat patiently waiting on my porch swing. Saturday mornings were set aside to take Nana's usual Saturday and Sunday dinners and baked goods to the shelter, and Tommy wanted to accompany me every chance he could. We were neighbors and had known each other since he was two and I was nine. Though he was half my size and seven years younger, he had always wanted to be my protector. But more than that, I could tell Tommy had a pure and deep love for me, like that of a brother. And so he waited, as he always did, smiling and swinging and listening for my footsteps to echo down the hallway of the first floor that led to the front door. He waited for the smell of my 'sweet scent', as he called it, to permeate the air that flowed gently, pushed by the humming window fan in the shed kitchen at the back of the house. He said I smelled like the fresh air of a peaceful and quiet day at the beach. I smiled when I thought about him. I was blessed to have such a dear little friend. As I opened the screen door, I laid the large handled bag of home cooking on the porch swing next to where Tommy sat, grinning from ear to ear.

"Ready?" I asked. " Did you eat Tommy?"

Tommy sniggled, as if he was the cat that ate the mouse.

I patted Tommy's back. "What's so funny?"

Tommy hugged my tummy tightly, with the top of his head measuring slightly under my rib cage.

"Here," I handed him a warm square of Nana's butter oozing banana bread.

Tommy looked directly into my eyes. "Thanks Andy." His eyes were filled with joy and he began to sing under his breath in a high pitched tone, "I know something you don't know I know..."

"What did you say, Tommy?" I asked and paused, smiling at his little boy grin. I shook my head as I picked up grandmom's cooking, carrying it on one arm. "Let's go, silly."

We walked hand in hand to the Community Shelter, both very quiet for our own special reasons. Tommy was at peace holding my hand, however, I was still somewhat in shock from narrowly escaping the crazed man at the train station last night. Police had brought down the man who was concentrating on my demise, but their strange hesitation made me question their motives. It definitely didn't allow me to trust them as law enforcement officers. Fortunately, it took no time for my faith to be reaffirmed and to realize that I was being protected by God and His armies to complete my mission. I knew no man could alter what God had planned for me.

"Tommy...have you..." I didn't quite know how to ask this without sounding like a lunatic. "Have you seen anything strange or different in my backyard?"

"Of course." Tommy answered with the utmost of confidence.

"Of course?" I was perplexed at his answer. "Well, what I mean is..."

"The cloud people," Tommy said very succinctly.

"Yes! Yes! The cloud people, Tommy. You've seen them?"

"Yep, we talk every day. They help me with my problems and I help them with theirs."

I felt bewildered and at a loss for words, but asked, "How do you help them, Tommy?"

"They give me different 'ssignments. Sometimes I do them by myself and sometimes with other ...people."

I paused, pinched my lips together between my teeth and said, "They gave me an assignment too."

"I know. You have to find your mom and dad and together unite families and tell people to believe," he said with certainty yet with a childlike impatience. And there was that smile again.

There was a long silence as we continued our walk to the shelter. *All this time, Tommy lived next door to me and he knew about all this?* I thought.

"I know where they are, Andy. I can take you to your mother and father."

"Tommy! You're just a little boy! And besides it would be way too dangerous for you." *Tommy was ten years old and like my little brother. No way could I jeopardize his life,* I thought. *And besides...how could he know?*

"Um. I'm not who you think I am, Andy."

This was all getting kind of weird. I stopped and looked at Tommy. "Well, who are you then?"

"I know people who can help get us in." Tommy was being evasive even though he seemed to be knowledgeable of the entire situation. I however, was finding it hard to believe that a fourth grader was going to help me accomplish the mission I'd been assigned to.

"For right now, all you need to know is that we can travel through the sub-basements into the catacombs under Zone C. We will find your mom and dad and we'll have help." Tommy was beginning to sound a little more grown than ten years old.

"So," he said, grabbing my hand, "follow me. We can get underground through one particular Zone B building bordering the doomed."

"Well now, wait a minute...wait here." I ran quickly into the shelter to deliver Nana's delicious meals to my friends in the kitchen and returned to my little mission guide, who was waiting patiently on the shelter steps. "Okay, Tommy?" I said, shrugging my shoulders in slight disbelief bordering on the edge of suspicion. "I'm ready."

CHAPTER TWELVE

THE PATH

"We live by faith, not by sight."2 Corinthians 5:7

THE SMITH-BERGDOF BUILDING HAD been closed down for five years since the New World Court mandates abolished all major businesses that refused to contribute eighty percent of their earnings to the good of the new government. Once a busy hub for processing tuna and other canned fish products, the building was now a health hazard, emitting the stench of decayed rotten fish. It was still pungently nauseous to all who traveled near. The filthy, fish blood stained walls and rooms full of once frozen containers of fish products remained alive with maggots throughout the closed plant. A hungry rat population continued to devour whatever remained edible, spreading disease to wherever the rodents found refuge. In that this building bordered both Zones B and the C Doomed area, the NWC considered this to be just another perfect and very efficient means to expedite the death of the doomed population. Therefore the New World Court couldn't be more than pleased to leave it standing.

"We have to go in here to get to my father?" I asked, squirming at the sight of things and holding my nose closed.

Tommy just motioned for me to follow him. We found some

torch lights at the entrance to the building and Tommy pulled out a box of matches from his pocket to light them.

"You shouldn't have matches, Tommy, you could hurt yourself!" I said, and then caught myself. I was beginning to wonder how old Tommy really was. He just looked at me.

"I knew we'd need them," he said with a slight sarcasm.

I followed Tommy as he led me down crowded, dark, damp and cold hallways filled with cutting tables and half-empty fish crates. I don't know if it was better feeling my way through or seeing this repulsive mess.

"Down this way, Andy." Tommy grabbed my arm as my balance shifted on the fish oil slick steps. "We have to go down three floors to the third sub-basement."

There was no doubt in my mind that he wasn't an average little boy but never in my wildest dreams would I have imagined that he would be my mission guide. But then, I guess I never would have imagined any of this.

As we descended the three flights of steps, Tommy warned me, "This won't be pleasant. We'll be entering the sewer system and we have to wade through a block long of three foot, putrid water. And it's a bit cold down here. I'm sorry, Andy. After that, we'll journey through the catacombs and we'll find your father there."

"You've been down here before, Tommy?"

Again evasive, Tommy said, "Look at the walls on your right side, Andy. See those hooks holding rubber over-the-shoulder pant boots?"

I placed my hands on the nasty, filthy, maggot-squirming walls and felt something slick. "Uhooh," I shuttered, I think I've found them."

"Well, grab two pairs, we're going to need them. This water isn't only dirty, it's toxic from government operations that drain into the sewer systems."

"So, you have been down here before, haven't you, Tommy?"

Tommy looked down to the ground, a bit annoyed and searched for the right words, "I just know the route."

CHAPTER THIRTEEN

ENDURING LIGHT

"You, O Lord, keep my lamp burning; my God turns my darkness into light." Psalm 18:28

OUR JOURNEY THROUGH THE old tuna plant brought us to a rather objectionable looking stairwell. I looked up to the skylight, seven floors above me and I welcomed the sunlight. Then I looked down at the descending darkness, the mysterious darkness, where we were to travel into the very depths of the earth. Darkness was half the fear, the other half was the small crawly creatures I could feel brushing past my feet and arms as I tried not to touch the walls. I prayed God was with us down here. There I was doing it again. If I was going to proceed in faith, I needed to discard my doubts right now and put my fears aside. I looked at Tommy and felt reassured that the cloud people had given me an excellent guide. The crawly things were a bit much when they fell into my hair though.

"I can do everything through Him who gives me strength, "[6] I kept telling myself over and over again. "There, now I feel better, much better. I'm fine now," I took three steps and I lost it. "Tommy, I'm afraid. Let's turn back." *Where did that come from, I thought I was fine. Wasn't that me talking to me? Can't stop now, this is my mission straight from God.* I shook my hands furiously like a pianist

getting ready for a concert. "Okay," I said, "let's...let's do this."

"He will never leave you, remember, Andy? Besides, we have company." Tommy turned around and pointed the torchlight to reflect on the wet floor. A faint vision of moving angelic-like bodies were hovering above us, appearing ready at any moment to intercede and protect. I felt a comforting brush of their wings against my shoulder.

"See, Andy, we'll be okay. God loves us. Remember, *you* have to believe, if you expect anyone else to. Now, c'mon."

CHAPTER FOURTEEN

ANSWERED PRAYER

"Delight yourself in the Lord and He will give you the desires of your heart." Psalm 37:4

"Who are you and why are you here?" An ice cold hand grabbed my shoulder from behind. Something very sharp was lodged in my back. It gave me a sickening feeling. I wanted to throw up, but I could hardly breathe. I stood motionless, my throat dry, my muscles frozen with fear.

"We're here to see Michael T," Tommy said. "We're here to give him a message. This is his daughter, Angeleigh. Now could you remove those knives, please?"

I shivered as the knife was released, and as the cold hand left my back.

"Turn around," the man said.

I raised my torchlight to see my offender. He stood near seven feet tall and had long stringy hair that reached his waist. He appeared to wear layers of sweat clothes, much needed to trap his body heat in this frigid and damp place. He held a knife with an ornate scrimshaw handle in one hand and a makeshift, unlit torch light in the other. His eyes were sinister, but in some odd way compassionate. He was accompanied by one other individual, equally frightening in appearance.

"How did you know to come here?" asked one of the men.

"Romulus knows me. Where is he?" Tommy retorted rather impatiently.

"We were given information of my father's whereabouts by my grandfather, Mr. Holbert Thriambeuo. Please, take us to my father!" I pleaded.

The man returned his blade to its waist holder and then moved forward into the dark. The men carried no flashlights. Their eyes must have become accustomed to the darkness from their time spent here.

"Very quickly, now. Follow us. Quickly, through here," one of the men told us.

We welcomed our passage out of the toxic sewer water to a hallway leading to yet another stairwell. I could feel the presence of others. This time I knew they were not our protectors, but instead perhaps other human prisoners of this darkness. I felt as if at any moment, the walls were going to become alive with beings walking toward us from all sides and we would need to battle for our lives as well as for the only oxygen lingering beneath our nostrils in these deep, dreadful depths of the earth. As we proceeded, we caught a glimpse of their shadows in my flickering torchlight. They were indeed giant creatures, perhaps not mortal and not to be paid attention to. And they were indeed watching our every move.

Tommy wrapped his hand tightly around mine. The tails of rats brushed my ankles as we stepped apprehensively. *Jesus, keep us safe*, I muttered uncontrollably and repetitiously.

"This way," one of the men directed.

I shined the torchlight to guide our footing and to keep from tripping over the dead vermin and debris. We came upon a tall wooden door secured with a large, heavy lock.

"Come now, we must safeguard our entrance." After passing

through and relocking the other side, heavy sandbags were placed for added weight protection against the insulation pads lining the door, upon which hung a large wooden cross.

Beyond the entrance was the opening to another world. A large room extending at least two city blocks was filled with the busyness of an old time newspaper office. People worked diligently at hundreds of computers, fax machines, laser printers and street monitors. Not new technology but apparently functional for their purposes. The man who brought us here called to a gentleman who seemed to be the head of this operation.

"Hey, Mike, there's someone here to see you."

That must be my father, I thought. *All these years and now he was just a few feet away.* My heart pounded and my palms began to sweat with impatience. I wondered how he would receive me. I wondered if at first sight, I would know he loved me and if I would recognize truth in his eyes. I had prayed for this moment for so long. This had been my dream since I was a little girl courting such fantasies that played in my head. Time stopped momentarily, teasing my anxious spirit. As he turned, I looked into his eyes and they were bathed in genuineness. It was him. I knew by his eyes, and his smile welcomed me as his long, lost daughter.

"Father!" I cried, falling into his arms for the first time in my life. Tears flowed and we held each other tightly. *My father! I was here with my father!* I had waited so long. I felt like I had a family. I felt accepted. I felt peace.

"My child, I knew one day you would come. Forgive me for leaving you," he said as he stepped back to look at me.

"I'm just happy I found you, Dad. I have looked into the eyes of every person in my presence since I was a little girl, in hopes I might find you," I said as I tried unsuccessfully to hold back the tears.

Tommy peeked around the back of me.

"Forgive me, Father. This is my good friend and little protector, Tommy."

"Yes, I know," said Dad, "and thank you for safeguarding her journey."

"You know Tommy, Father?" I stood perplexed.

"Angeleigh, I've been tracking your whereabouts for many years, but I couldn't come to the surface and risk our mission. Tommy has been my liaison to your existence."

"Seems I've been the outsider here, huh," I said feeling a bit awkward.

"You couldn't have known until you were ready," my father said as he hugged me tightly. "But you're ready now. And you have to be strong."

"Hmm, I've been told that before," I replied. "Oh, and grandfather, he has told me much about you."

"I haven't seen father in a very long time. He's well, is he?"

"Yes, and he spoke very highly of you, Dad."

"My father is very dear to me. He told me about Jesus and gave me my first Bible, but I wasn't a serious student of the Word. A bit too headstrong. For a short time, I was even led astray to live the fast life. Thank God my dad never gave up on me. He convinced me to follow the true purpose I was given on this earth." Michael smiled. "So I started studying the Word and praying and God revealed to me the leadership that my family down here needs."

My heart suddenly felt empty. *I was his family.*

"I know what you're thinking, Angeleigh, but it's my calling to lead this mission for God's family. We are all His children on this earth."

One of my dad's assistants approached him from behind.

"Michael, there's a problem concerning tonight's mission. I need to speak to you right away." My father nodded and grabbed my arm, leading me through the crowded room.

"I must attend to business, child," said my Dad.

"But, I've looked for you for so long," I said in desperation.

"And now you've found me and look at the big family you've

acquired." My dad took my hand in his. "Calm down, Angeleigh, we will always be together from this point on."

"But Dad, I don't want to go," I pleaded. "I want to talk about things. So much has happened and..."

"You're just going to your room to get cleaned up and Maria will give you something good to eat." Dad motioned to Maria, a kindly old lady in her seventies. "Please Maria, get these children settled and fed."

"But, Dad..."

"No buts. Here..." My father placed a beautiful gold locket in the shape of a cross in my hand. "I've wanted to give this to you for a very long time. Now clean up, eat and relax. I have a few loose ends to attend to. I love you, Angeleigh. And welcome to Mission City," said my father as he disappeared into the sea of working people.

"Come, youngsters," said Maria, leading us very slowly, with cane in hand, and limping from the apparent arthritis in her hips. She brought us to a quaint little room, fully equipped with a corner chair; two mirrored tables with basins, two towels and two soap dishes; a bureau of drawers filled with fresh clean clothes in our sizes; two small flashlights; a framed print on the wall of a family relaxing on a beach of long ago; a beautiful hand-painted, four-paneled screen so I could change my clothes in private; and two amply blanketed fold-up cots.

"You may rest here, children." Her voice was soft and sweet and made me homesick for Nana. "I will bring food," Maria said as she hobbled out the room.

Tommy opened the bureau drawers to select some dry clothes.

"Here Ang," he said as he placed a sweatshirt, T-shirt, pants and sneakers on my cot, "maybe we should wash up."

"Stinky, huh?"

"Yep, and these boots have enough toxins on them to eat us alive."

Tommy moved the screen in front of one table and basin. "You wash up and change, Ang. I'll just sit over here and quickly get cleaned up."

I smiled at Tommy's thoughtfulness.

"Happy to see your dad, Angie?"

"Yes!" I felt a lump in my throat and got quiet. "But, Tommy, my dad, he wasn't trying to avoid me, was he?" I began to feel pressure in my head as my eyes welled with tears. I just couldn't hold it in any longer. "He just couldn't jeopardize his mission, like he said, right? I mean, he really does love me, doesn't he, Tommy?" I finished washing and started putting on my clothes as I tried to put my heartache into words. "It's just that I've spent seventeen years wondering why my parents hated me so much. My grandfather said they left to protect me. But, now I'm here and my Dad doesn't want to talk to me!"

"Andy, yes, your parents love you," Tommy said reassuringly. "Your father is a busy man, but you will be together for the rest of your lives."

I came from behind the screen and shook my head in agreement. "Thank you for bringing me here, Tommy. I owe it all to you."

"Andy, don't ever forget that you are on a mission. I am your helper and that's all. I have a mission just like you."

We sat to rest after our arduous journey. My cot felt like a mountain of cotton balls and was comforting as my body was aching from the damp and cold, especially after wading through the sewer water. I picked up and examined the precious locket that my father had given me. It was in the shape of a Trinity cross. I carefully opened its tiny compartment within its beautiful gold filigree border and read the engraving inside – "'*Live by the Spirit.*'[7] '*Love, Joy, Peace, Patience, Kindness, Goodness, Faithfulness, Gentleness and Self-Control.*'"[8] A comforting sense of assurance came over me.

"The Fruits of the Spirit," I said.

"What did you say, Andy?"

"The words in my locket, they're the Fruits of the Spirit."

"Yes, and they're also the cloud people," Tommy replied nonchalantly while he bounced lightly on his soft cot mattress.

"You're right, Tommy. Do you think my father knows?"

"Oh, I'm certain of it."

"Hmm...," I thought for a minute, "Tommy, do you always have to go to them? I mean, do the cloud people ever come to you?"

"Well, sure, but it depends on you. You know...if you accept their presence. They don't want to scare you. And besides they're always with you. You just don't recognize them when you're living in doubt, you know...when you're not a true believer."

"Hmm," I nodded my head, looking back at the locket.

"How did you know where to find him, Tommy? How could you know where my dad was?"

"The Spirit...the cloud people, they told me. And they will instruct you as well. But Andy, you have to learn to listen."

"Yes, I know, the cloud people told me that too." I felt confused. "I just don't know what I'm listening for and if it's me talking to myself."

"You should pray more. Ask God to help you to discern His voice. You need to truly believe in order to keep open the portal that connects you to our Heavenly Father. There are many treasures awaiting believers, as well as many closed doors to the unconvinced."

"But Tommy..." A faint knocking on the outside wall interrupted me.

"Angeleigh, it's Dad." My father entered smiling. "I just wanted to say it's good to have you here and to see how you were doing before I go back to work. We have a big mission in just a few hours."

"We're fine, Dad. It's very comfortable down here." Dad hugged me and shook Tommy's hand.

"Well, if there's anything you need, we're all family here."

"One thing, Dad," I paused. "The past few days have been very strange. People appear and then they disappear and these black shadows seem to follow me everywhere. You probably think I'm imagining things." I shook my head and looked to the ground, feeling rather foolish.

"On the contrary, Angeleigh," said Dad as he sat down in the corner chair. "You see you've entered a whole new realm of existence. You're recognizing what unbelievers can't see. But just remember this. Fear is a tool used by the enemy. Realizing your fear is the first step. Faith is the opposite of fear. Replace your fear with faith. Remember- "*Whoever listens to Me will live in safety and be at ease, without fear of harm.*"[9] Proverbs 1:33. Stay in the Word, Angeleigh. Many of the mysteries of God are revealed there. "

Just then, there was a knock on the outside wall of the room.

"It's Maria," announced her sweet voice, "I have your supper. Can I come in?"

"Oh, here she is," said Dad as he stood up to leave the room. "I shall see you both tomorrow. Rest well. I love you."

Maria had her hands full as she carried in a tray of steaming food that consisted of two bowls of creamy chicken noodle with carrot soup, two large hamburgers, two bananas, two buttered danishes and two containers of milk. My eyes widened as she placed what reminded me of nana's cooking before us.

"You look so surprised, children," Maria exclaimed. "We eat well down here. I love to cook and we have plenty of people who love to eat my food!" Maria laughed and her tummy shook.

"But, how do you have such fresh foods down here?" I asked.

"All this food is made from fruits and vegetables! Hydroponics, dear! We have a special room with extra sensitive plant lighting and climate control. We grow award winners! Very nutritious!"

Maria smiled with much pride and threw her hands up in the air. "I'm a gardener as well as a chef!" Then Maria swiftly clapped her hands and said, "¡Buen apetito! In Spanish that means 'Happy eating!' Enjoy youngsters. We are so pleased you have joined us." She walked out the room waddling, her stature short and wide.

Tommy and I ate that night like we hadn't eaten in years. As we delighted in our meal, we got a bit sleepy in the process. We talked about all the fun things we did as we were growing up and we talked about our journey ahead of us. I knew that my journey would test my strength. *What a blessing to know Jesus,* I thought, "*the author and perfecter of our faith.*" **10**

CHAPTER FIFTEEN

ONSLAUGHT

"Death and Destruction are never satisfied." Proverbs 27:20

A LOUD CRASH AND the sounds of electrical equipment being broken startled us. Troubled, we looked at each other as we heard a voice yelling, "No, what are you doing! Michael!" Multiple gun shots ensued. I was about to look out the door when Tommy pulled me back.

"Don't be foolish, Andy. There's nothing you can do."

"But my father!" I cried.

"Your father can take care of himself. We, on the other hand, have to hide." Tommy looked around. "Come on," he said as he took my hand and pulled me in through a slight opening at the rear of the room where the particle board walls were warped, leaving a hardly noticeable hiding space. We crawled into a very dark cubbyhole. The rampage continued and seemed endless. Holding each other tight, we silently prayed. After what seemed to be an eternity, the conflict ended, but I didn't trust the silence. My fear and frustrations were weakening me. We waited, holding each other. We waited and waited for what seemed to be many hours. Then from sheer exhaustion, I fell into a deep sleep.

CHAPTER SIXTEEN

EVER-PRESENT MESSENGERS

"The weapons we fight with are not the weapons of the world." 2 Corinthians 10:4

FOR A SPLIT SECOND I forgot where I was. The sunlight streaming through my sheer bedroom curtains usually woke me every morning. But there was nothing but darkness and an unearthly silence around me. I felt Tommy's shoulder against mine and nudged him but he appeared sound asleep. I crawled through the wallboards and felt my way to the bureau of drawers where I found one of the flashlights. Cradling its nose in my palms to dim the light when I turned it on, I apprehensively surveyed first our room and then the main room outside. The carnage caused me to vomit. Bodies lay everywhere. The room where dad had preached that afternoon and all that was in it was destroyed. I felt a hand on my back and I almost passed out. It was Tommy.

"My father is dead!" I began weeping uncontrollably. I fell to my knees and Tommy knelt down beside me.

"No... they took him," Tommy explained. "The people that did this, they want to take over. They need your father for information. He's a brilliant man, Angie. His methods of leadership and development are unprecedented. He's safe, at least for a while."

"Well, we have to go find him, Tommy. I can't lose him again!" I began to stand as Tommy pulled me back to my kneeling position on the floor.

"Hold it, Andy. We don't know where we're going." Tommy rubbed my shoulder. "We have to pray for guidance and direction first. Always pray first." He took my hand, we bowed our heads and Tommy led us in prayer.

"Direct our paths, Dear Lord, We humbly ask for guidance. In Jesus' Name, we pray. Amen."

We sat in silence for a long time, waiting on Him. Then before us appeared the most majestic vision I have ever seen. Translucent figures, perhaps one hundred in number, hovered before us. They were very tall in stature, dressed in white robes with gold cords at their waists. Their hair was long and tied back with the same type of gold cord. Their wings made of thousands of wisplike feathers, undulated gently as if suspended in water. Their spirit illuminated them. Some stood ready for battle with breastplates and swords, others were in prayer and still others watched and waited, as if instructions were being sent. Then the most radiant presence appeared. He was the most grand in stature. Wearing a breastplate of shimmering gold, he held his arms up to the heavens. Above him, as if made of glittering diamonds, emerged the sign of the cross. We watched in awesome wonder. I felt so blessed to experience such a site.

"That's it, Tommy," I said with relief, "the sign of the cross. We must go to the mission house. My father will be there." I was getting stronger and knew I was protected by the angels of God. We were being prepared to fight this new world regime and remind God's children that the Spirit of the Lord lives strong in each one of us, if only we will believe.

CHAPTER SEVENTEEN

WAGER

"Love must be sincere. Hate what is evil; cling to what is good." Romans 12:9

MEANWHILE...

"I'm telling you, they'll be here. But, we just have to get that little messenger boy away from her."

"So, this won't be a problem?"

"Don't worry...I've got it all under control. That parasite has stuck to her like glue for seven years. We gotta loosen that glue is all. And she'll do anything to see me again. Besides, she thinks she's saving me. It's practically done."

"So, you'll end her life this week."

"Like I said, it's practically done."

The New World Court officials, left the room, one by one, with Major Hunt pausing. "Michael T," he said, "Know this, if you don't resolve this, you both die."

The door slammed behind them.

Michael T was accustomed to making deals throughout his life, but never before had he jeopardized a life other than his. He was playing the NWC at the expense of his daughter and he wondered how far his deceit would go.

CHAPTER EIGHTEEN

OBSTACLES

"Be strong and courageous. Do not be afraid or ter-rified because of them, for the Lord your God goes with you; He will never leave you nor forsake you. "
Deuteronomy 31:6

"So, we'll go to the mission house," I told Tommy. "God gave us the sign of the cross above the angels and this necklace from my father, to instruct me."

"Very good, Andy," Tommy replied. "Now you're learning. But this could be very dangerous you know," he said as if to test me.

"We have God on our side. No man can interfere."

Tommy nodded his head in confidence and grabbed the flash-lights. "Let's be on our way then. I think I know a shortcut out of here."

By squeezing out the back of the same cubbyhole we had slept in, we were able to make our way through a narrow hallway con-necting supply rooms and leading to the other end of the main business room, where an escape door was mysteriously left open.

"This is where the intruders must have broken in," I told Tom-my.

"Probably," Tommy replied and pointed. "There Andy, we have

to climb those steps over there."

I walked over to them and looked up the narrow hole we had to climb through. "I hear somebody up there," I whispered.

Tommy gave me that look and I knew this would be another adventure. "Hmm...some of the doomed people," he said nonchalantly. "They're known as the Wickeds."

I didn't want to ask, but I had to know. "Okay," I sighed. "Why are they called the Wickeds, Tommy?"

"They're some of the doomed that were exposed to too many toxins," he said shaking his head rather casually and his voice sort of changed to a high pitch as he further explained. "It just...sort of...changed them in many ways. You know, it changed their brain functions, their skin color, their looks." Then he mumbled so I could hardly understand a word. "Their teeth grew long, they grew extra parts and..." Tommy hesitated and looked to the ground in an effort to find the right words. "And they like people. Actually, they like to eat them. There, I said it. They like to eat people."

I turned around and immediately headed back the way we came.

"Andy, no, stop. C'mon now." Tommy dropped his shoulders as if he was tired of trying to convince me of the surety of faith. "It'll be okay."

"God will help us but He didn't tell us to be stupid!" I whispered angrily.

"Well, we've got to get out of here," Tommy grumbled, annoyed at my negativity. "So, just follow me." My little friend climbed first and I stayed about three steps behind him. "Come up here. Look at this," Tommy whispered. Two of the Wickeds were sitting at a table not ten feet from where we hid from view. I felt like a fish begging for a hook to snare me. The Wickeds were playing a game of cards and drinking their favorite homemade ale made from distilled toxic spray liquid that was available for purchase on the black market. An old hurricane lamp illuminated their strange abode. Old cracked tires, elbow pipes chained together like a giant bracelet, a set of stairs leading to nowhere, dozens of cases marked creamed herring strewn with burlap bags, and a pillow or two fashioning their means to rest, comprised their odd furnishings. They were dirty, miserable looking souls and their conversation was extremely disturbing.

"Me hungry... Whatchoo got 'round here t'eat, Misou? " asked the fattest Wicked to his friend.

"You got people? ...Me love people." And they both let out big bolts of laughter exposing their rotting purple teeth.

"I think we can outrun them," Tommy whispered. "They look pretty intoxicated already." Tommy peaked above the floorboards once more. The two were laughing heartily, one falling out of his chair. Tommy scanned the room for the exits that would lead us to the surface of Zone B. On his right, only visible to those who believe, an angel pointed to the correct exit.

"I see the way and we have help." Tommy pointed to our holy messenger. "We have to be swift. On three, Andy, follow me on three. One...Two..."

If I didn't know better, I'd have thought we flew up the steps because I don't remember touching them along the way. We went straight for the exit. The Wickeds, of course, followed us while grumbling inaudible chewing sounds. It was two hundred feet or so before we reached another staircase. To my surprise, the Wickeds were incredibly swift creatures and I could feel them grabbing at the heels of my feet as we climbed. The stairwell brought us up to the tracks of an old underground subway stop where fortunately we were able to gain a lead of about twenty feet as we ran, searching for any means of escaping from them. I grabbed Tommy's hand, pulling him close to me, trying to safe-guard him from these awful cannibals. But one of the Wickeds gained speed, ran right up to Tommy and pulled him so hard that his small body pummeled against the concrete walls of the tunnel. Then it grabbed his other arm and with its' razor sharp teeth, tore a chunk from Tommy's skin. It took all I had to hold Tommy and keep going. Just as their extraordinary strength was beginning to overcome ours, a warm hand grabbed me and quickly pulled us through a subway tunnel doorway, closing and securing it behind us.

"Maria!" I screamed. "What a welcome sight! You're alive!"

"Yes, child. We narrowly escaped with our lives. It was pretty bad." She showed us her arms and legs still covered in blood. "Very unfortunate as you can see. The New World Court Death Squad took many. So many died. So many injured. Some of us are gathering medical supplies now to treat the wounded and we're beginning our exile to safe hiding," Maria said, as she held on to the wooden cross that she wore around her neck. "We couldn't find you two. You weren't in your beds." Maria hugged us tightly. "It's good to know you're safe."

"Yes ma'am, when we heard gunshots, we found a hiding place and fell asleep, I guess out of fear and exhaustion," I said. "I'm sorry, we couldn't do anything to help."

"You two youngsters would have no defense against these evil monsters." Maria noticed Tommy's wound. "I need to attend to that arm, little one."

A large piece of skin was hanging off Tommy's arm. He was losing a good deal of blood at this point, making his body quite weak. Maria tore a large strip of cloth from her sleeve to wrap the wound tightly and stop the bleeding.

"I'll be fine, Maria," said Tommy.

"You should rest. Have some soup. Regain your strength."

"The bleeding has stopped now." Tommy removed the cloth to reveal the skin back in place and a closed wound. "See?"

Maria couldn't believe her eyes. "Maybe you do have friends in high places."

"Yes, Maria," Tommy acknowledged. "Now we must be on our way to find Andy's father."

"You know where your father is, child?" asked Maria.

"We believe we can find him at the 30th St. Mission House. My grandfather is there as well and there's much we all have to talk about," I said.

"Well, God be with you, children," said Maria as she hugged each of us. "If you follow that hallway on your left, you will reach a maintenance room. About fifty feet from there, you will find stairs that will take you to the surface, not far from 30th Street. Be safe."

CHAPTER NINETEEN

STUMBLING BLOCKS

"The night is nearly over; the day is almost here. So let us put aside the deeds of darkness and put on the armor of light." Romans 13:12

WE FOLLOWED MARIA'S DIRECTIONS which brought us four blocks away from the mission house. I held my arm around Tommy's waist, helping to support him as we walked. By now I had no doubt that Tommy was not of this world. And though his arm had miraculously healed, his strength hadn't fully returned to his earthly body, causing him to move painfully. I took a quick glimpse of our location. It was early morning and so far this route wasn't as spooky as my first visit here, though I was still weary of lurking creatures behind dark doorways. I knew they were out there. They seemed to follow me constantly these days. I knew they were there to discourage me, to make me doubt myself, my mission and mostly my faith in God. That was their job, but God had a greater purpose for me and my faith was getting stronger with every victory over fear, with every passing trial. Upon reaching 30th St. Mission, I stopped at the foot of the steps to catch my breath before making the climb. The door of the mission opened and there stood my father.

"There's my smart little girl," he said rather sarcastically.

What a welcome site to see my dad! I helped Tommy make the climb and as soon as we reached the landing and entered the front door, we were grabbed from behind. I felt a hand over my mouth and an arm tightly gripping my shoulder. A man pulled Tommy out of my arms. I tried to tell him to be careful, that Tommy wasn't well, but the man's hand clenched tighter over my lips. I was led into the main office where he pushed me down into a chair.

"Tommy's hurt. You have to help him," I pleaded to my father.

"Oh, we'll take good care of him. You won't have to worry about him anymore." Suddenly my father didn't seem like the same person that I'd met back at Mission City, the same person that had shown me truth and love.

"Don't you hurt him, father!" I yelled as I attempted to stand, but was immediately shoved back into my seat.

"Relax little girl. Now why would I hurt your little friend," said my father in a sinister tone. "In fact, he can come with when we go to get your mother."

"Daddy, we're going for mom? You know where she is?" I was confused over his brash actions but the thought of rescuing my mother made me naively trust him again.

"Of course, but I need you to wait for me while I once again take care of some unfinished business. Daddy's a busy man, little girl." Michael T walked over to the glass key case on the wall, opened it and removed a very antique looking key.

"Come my dear, you can wait in my old room down the hall," said my Dad. Once we left the office, my father appeared to be in an awful hurry. I didn't know him very well, so I couldn't understand his changing moods, but the look in his eyes was very preoccupied and troubled. And instead of going down the hall, he almost pushed me down a flight of steps. Then we walked a few feet through a short hallway and stopped. "Right about here," said dad. I watched as my father stooped down, lifted a small floorboard and pulled a lever beneath it, releasing the walls to open a secret passageway. "Step in, my child," said dad. "This is a safe room, no one will find you here. Those men that kidnapped me want to hurt you as well."

"Who are those men, Dad? Did they hurt you? And how do they know me?"

"I'll answer all your questions in good time. You just stay in here. There's food and a place to rest. I'll be back soon." And with that, he quickly closed the door and proceeded to lock it.

"But Dad..."

"Really young lady, relax. And try to be quiet, I'll be back. I love you," he said as he quickly secured the secret door.

I could hear dad's footsteps walking up to the office. I heard loud voices arguing. It was hard to hear all that was being said, but my dad was asking for more time. Then I heard him clearly say, "But that's my father!" A loud gunshot frightened me and I moved back away from the door until I reached the wall and then fell to the floor into a squat position. I felt like I was being consumed by fear once again. I felt like I was on the verge of being defeated. *Faith, Angeleigh, Faith,* I told myself. Those who are the most valuable to you always make you the most vulnerable. *But what had they done to my father? My grandfather? What were they doing to Tommy?* I tried not to fear for my life. I didn't know if I could really trust my father. I thought about Nana. I wanted to go home. I thought about how she must be going out of her mind with worry. It had been days since I'd seen her and I never, ever, would want to hurt or worry grandmom. I lowered my head against my knees and tried to stop shaking. "My trust is in the Lord, He'll never leave me," I prayed quietly.

"Andy," spoke a nearby voice.

I slowly raised my head. In the dimly lit room, across from me on a couch, sat Tommy! I rushed over to him, embracing his small frame.

"You're alright?"

"I'm fine. The men have left. But your grandfather... they shot him and he's in the office upstairs. We have to go to him. He hasn't much time." Tommy took my hand. "They thought they could stop me, but they don't know much about beings like me."

"Who are you Tommy? Are you my guardian angel?"

"I'm your protector. Come now before the men return looking for you."

Tommy pressed a button on the wall to release the lock and open the door. We raced up the steps to the main office only to see my grandfather lying on the floor, bleeding, holding his chest, and taking labored breaths.

"Oh grandfather," I cried, falling to my knees at his side.

"Child...no time...they're after your mother...they know...she's an important key to your mission. Before they find her..." My grandfather was choking on the blood that was filling his lungs. "You have to get to her before they do, child."

"I don't know how to find mother," I cried in anguish as I held my grandfather's head up to allow the blood to flow away from his throat. "Grandfather," I pleaded, "Hold on."

"Your mother...go up to the hill country, near the Wiskonset River...follow ... follow the river." My grandpa was beginning to lose consciousness. "Follow the river upstream...till you notice a sign...it says plateau 150 feet ...cross the river...then climb high into the woods, child. God...God be...with...you."

"Grandpa!" I cried.

"Biosphere Six. Go, go, child. I see...Jesus. I see a beautiful...Light." My grandfather was gone.

I screamed, holding him tightly in my arms. "God, why are you taking everyone away from me!"

"Andy," Tommy was trying to comfort me.

"Leave me alone, I don't want consolation right now. I want people to stop leaving me!"

Tommy sat patiently while I let out my grief. We prayed and as I held my grandfather, I believe I could feel his spirit leave his body. I knew he was safe and in the loving arms of Jesus now. I bowed my head and reverently thanked God for the place He had prepared for him.

"I'm sorry, Tommy, I'm sorry," I said as I paused to compose myself. "I suppose we need to go now. We always have to go."

"Yes, much of our journey still lies ahead of us."

Tommy felt my sadness, but he knew at this moment, that the one living God was offering reassurance and strength. Hope couldn't leave me, not anymore. There will always be setbacks. Forces will always try to discourage me. That's how it is when you follow Christ. But God doesn't give you any more to bear than you can handle. And He would bring me through this.

"I'll be okay I…I'll be alright, Tommy," I said with a smile. "From this point on, I move in faith."

CHAPTER TWENTY

MOUNTAINS

"You will be secure, because there is hope; you will look about you and take your rest in safety." Job 11:18

WE HAD TO TRAVEL underground as far as possible for safety's sake. Though they might start looking for us, the NWC Police didn't bother investigating the catacombs. They would wait until we surfaced. Our next step was to find a vehicle to take us up to the hill country and Biosphere Six. It was pretty rough terrain and not having much driving experience created another obstacle. However, I knew there was no time for doubt. Tommy couldn't drive, he could barely see over the steering wheel. That put me in the driver's seat. And the only person I knew that owned a car was Mrs. Woodrow. Fortunately, our journey through the underground catacombs was heading in the direction of her neighborhood. Unfortunately, the exit closest to Mrs. Woodrow's house, first took us into above ground doomed territory, just thirty feet or so past free Zone B. If seen, we would be target practice. As we carefully peaked out the abandoned Zone C train depot, we noticed the area was laden with heavy surveillance. That would be our first obstacle to defeat. Because of the restrictions enforced on non-interzone travel, if you were caught, it wouldn't be pretty.

Monitors canvassed every inch of the street, criss-crossing their spy beams. High above the ground, an armed guard stationed in his platform office, carefully observed any measure of activity on the scanning screens. This wasn't going to be easy. The only chance we had was to distract the guard for at least five seconds while we ran for freedom to Zone B. By the time we sneaked our way through and were noticed on the reconnaissance replay, we should be long gone. We knew we would be put on the Terminal Transgressor List to be shot on site when found, but at least we would be buying a little time. So we hid from the windows of the depot for safety while strategizing our escape.

"Only thirty feet, but we can't be seen or we'll be dead," I told Tommy. I knew we would make it across, the question was how. We looked around the deserted train depot for resources and I noticed an old circuit breaker on the wall.

"Tommy, look here. Let's just shut off the power to the street lights and we can make a run for it."

"Angie, that's not enough to distract them. It's a little overcast out there but it's just not dark enough. They'll notice us. But the streetlights," Tommy rubbed his chin as he thought. "See that light adjacent to the guard station? I need to break it, you know, shatter it and make a loud disturbance. That will distract them long enough for you to get to safety."

"What do you mean so I can get to safety? And what are you going to do, Tommy? I'm not going without you! I can't lose anyone else!"

"Don't worry about me, I'll be fine and I'll be right behind you. We have no time to argue, Angie." Tommy walked over to the circuit box and broke off the rusty Y-shaped handle.

"What can you do with that? Throw it at them?" I remarked sarcastically.

Tommy looked at me like I was the ten year old. "No, I had a friend once who rid himself of a giant in his life with something like this. Now do me a favor and pull out the band of elastic in the bottom of your pant leg."

I gave him a strange look, but didn't ask any questions. I ripped open the side seam of my left pant leg and slit the elastic band with a piece of metal that I found lying on the ground. It pulled out easy and I handed it to Tommy. He tied one end to the right bar and the other end to the left bar of the metal handle fashioning a sling shot of sorts. Then he found a large piece of concrete that had fallen out of the crumbling walls of the depot.

"Tommy, you had a friend who used a sling shot on a giant?" I laughed. "You know that reminds me of a Bible story..."

"Yep," Tommy interrupted, "but that was a long time ago. Alright Andy, as soon as you hear the glass break, you run. Understand? On the count of three," Tommy grabbed my hand. "You can do this. I'll be with you on the other side." Tommy got into position with a clear view of the streetlamp. I hid behind the exit door, ready to run.

"Okay Andy ...one...two...."

The glass broke and a loud burst of exploding electricity was my cue. I ran as fast as I could until I reached the free zone, but Tommy was nowhere in site. Some of the doomed people on the other side of the perimeter were watching me. I motioned to them to leave before they were blamed for the disturbance and shot. The government made it very clear that they were expendable and the only reason they lived was to save bullets. The government also relied on their poor health to do them in soon enough. There was still no sign of Tommy, so I inched my way back around the building to get a clear view of the street and I could see three policemen throwing my little friend into the back of a truck. I backed away from view and leaned against the building, breathing nervously. There was nothing I could do right now to help him. I didn't want to leave him, but I knew it was just me and Jesus now. I had to get to Mrs. Woodrow's home. My rescue list was getting longer and longer - my mother, my father, and now Tommy.

CHAPTER TWENTY-ONE
TRUST

"You will keep in perfect peace him whose mind is
steadfast, because he trusts in You."
Isaiah 26:3

THE YEARS FOLLOWING 2090 were disastrous. It was just as the
Bible said it would be. The world was all about self, vanity and
greed. There was no privacy. You could trust no one. A handful of
people proclaimed their allegiance to God and theirs was a fight
to the death. Everyone was guilty even if proven innocent. You
avoided anything that would draw attention to yourself. Earth was
in turmoil. Large-scale natural disasters obliterated island countries and desolated the coastlines of the major political powers,
giving new borders to fight for. The collapse of buildings and over-
flowing waterways created more destruction. The world was in a
perpetual state of chaos. So, in an effort to remedy the situation,
people turned to themselves and a group of resolute vigilantes
came together to create a new world power. This started out being
for the good of the people, but when mankind follows his own
directives instead of his Creator's, all things lead to self-satisfy-
ing power and corruption. And so ensued the destruction of the
family, of communities, of the nation, of the world. The New

World Court was formed. There were no longer countries but divisions, Zones A, B, and C within each of 29 Regions around the globe. Reconstruction of terrain was imperative and scientists following the emerging New World Court political party (of which there was no real choice to do otherwise), developed laboratory prototypes to replace nature. It wasn't long until these fiberglass botanicals were instituted in choice areas of each region and Mrs. Woodrow's neighborhood was one of those test sites. New World Court Technical Institutes were built globally to train subservient artists in prototype field engineering. The nonliving replications of God's handwork that were produced had multiple purposes. Beside blasphemy against God's creations, they were comfortable environments for ungodly spirits. Once again, I could feel them watching me, the dark shadows, the slithering dark shadows, imperceptible to many but not to me. They were all around me. They were comfortable in their sacrilegious domain. Thank God they hadn't invaded my neighborhood yet, where it was still hospitable to God's angels. Nervously, I made my way to Mrs. Woodrow's home, all the while anticipating government officials to be trailing me. I had roughly two more blocks to travel and with Tommy apprehended, I knew my arrest wouldn't be far behind. I felt a great sense of relief when I located Mrs. Woodrow's home on the next block, her car in her back driveway. *That's a bit odd,* I thought. *Why wouldn't she park her car in the garage where the sprayings wouldn't ruin the finish.* The lights were on inside the house, which hopefully meant she was home. I looked at my watch. It was seven minutes till noon which meant I needed shelter fast. I rang the front door bell but there was no answer, so I proceeded to the back door where I knocked loudly and called for her by name. I turned the doorknob but it was locked. I made my way back around the front of the house, looking through all the windows for some signs of my teacher. Through the curtains of the dining room, I saw Kyra sleeping on the couch. I knocked on the window as hard as I could, but she wasn't responding. I tried the front door, but that was locked. So, I looked for a rock, broke the window and climbed in.

"Kyra!" I shouted as I shook her furiously. "Kyra!" I checked her pulse. *O, thank you Lord, she's alive.* I shook her again and she started talking gibberish.

"Go.....you......no. NO!" Kyra was screaming at the top of her lungs. I held her tightly, trying to comfort her in her delirium. She continued screaming and then passed out. The spraying alarms began sounding their screeching sirens. I positioned a small throw pillow against the hole in the window, that I caused when I used the rock to break in, and then closed the drapes to conceal my presence and keep out the lethal spray. I made myself comfortable for the next four hours as I prayed for answers. I prayed for direction. I prayed Kyra would come out of this alive.

CHAPTER TWENTY-TWO

DO NOT BE TROULED

"Peace I leave with you; My peace I give you. I do not give to you as the world gives. Do not let your hearts be troubled and do not be afraid." John 14:27

As TIRED AS I was, I should have slept. I should have passed out from the sheer stress of all that I'd been through. But instead, I sat still, staring into space for the four hours that Kyra endured an agonizing sleep. I had plenty of time for prayer and it was exactly what I needed to comfort me. *Lord, I'm confused and tired. I've lost three people and possibly four if Kyra won't wake. But I'm not afraid anymore. I guess that's a good thing. I've learned that praying for guidance is a comfort that assures me, reminds me, that I'm not in charge. I've learned that when You give someone a mission, You give them all the help they need to accomplish it. But without Tommy, can you please tell me how to find the hill country? In Jesus' Name, I pray, Lord. Amen.*

I decided to make a pot of hot herbal tea and returned to Kyra, cradling her in my arms. She started to move slightly. She fought me as she woke, though I don't believe she knew it was me. Her reactions were jerky, her eyelids heavy.

"It's me Kyra, it's Angeleigh," I said softly so as not to startle her.

"Can you tell me what happened to you?"

Kyra was having difficulty forming words. In one garbled sentence, she said, "drug..me, teacher..took." I didn't know what she had been given or by whom, but from my work at the shelter, she seemed to be reacting from a very strong narcotic. She struggled to regain consciousness as if she was battling with unseen spirits. Her aggression was affecting her breathing and she began to cough up thick green phlegm. As I wiped her mouth clean, she grabbed my hand and began to respond.

"The New World Court, they want...total control, no unity, no families, Ang. They, they... created the virus, they make you think the virus is out of control!" Kyra grabbed my shoulders and pulled herself up into a sitting position, her confusion was leaving her now, her nausea beginning to clear.

"Angie, they number the water bottles. They add the virus to certain bottles, so they can control certain people. It's awful." Kyra coughed from deep in her lungs and then grabbed my shirt collar, "And they want you! You've got to be careful. They want you because you're causing trouble."

"Like my father," I mumbled.

"What?" Kyra asked as she lay back down.

"Here...take a sip of tea. Now, take it slow and tell me exactly what happened. And what on earth are you doing here?" I asked.

Kyra sipped her tea slowly. As it began to further clear her thoughts, she was able to explain. "Mrs. Woodrow called me at home. I'd just returned from visiting my cousin." Kyra took a few more sips of her hot drink, rubbed her eyes and yawned. "Mrs. Woodrow was worried sick about you because you hadn't contacted her for some supplies or something that you'd talked about. And she had called your grandmother who was frantic because she hadn't seen you for two and a half weeks."

"Two and a half weeks! I couldn't have been gone that long!"

"Ang, I've been at my cousins since June 23rd. Today is... July

14th, I think," Kyra said rubbing her eyes. "Well anyway, Mrs. Woodrow asked me to come over. We were going to look for you. Nana was going to contact the Misplaced Citizens Bureau, but Mrs. Woodrow advised her against it."

"Thank goodness for Mrs. Woodrow," I replied. "Nana doesn't know much about this new government of ours."

"Well anyway," Kyra continued, "when I came over, the police were here and they were yelling at Mrs. Woodrow."

"About what?" I asked.

"I don't know. Something about making copies of something. When I walked in the door, they stopped talking. And the next thing I knew, they were giving me a shot in my arm. But before the drug took effect, I heard them talking about the virus and Mrs. Woodrow was arguing about how they were killing innocent people with the water. Then they tied her hands and threw her in their car. I couldn't stop them Ang." Kyra started crying. "I couldn't stop them from taking her!" Kyra began shaking furiously and repeating over and over, "I don't know where they took her, Angie, I don't know where they took her."

"It's going to be okay Kyra. I have a fair idea of where they went." I looked around the room and then asked, "Have any idea where Mrs. Woodrow keeps her car keys?"

CHAPTER TWENTY-THREE

REFUGE IN HIM

*"If you make the Most High your dwelling, even the
Lord who is my refuge – then no harm will befall you,
no disaster will come near your tent." Psalm 91:9-10*

I STARTED THE CAR twice and it made that awful grinding noise. It was obvious I didn't know how to drive, but I guess I would have my chance to learn quickly. Kyra and I looked at each other and laughed. It was good to see my friend back to her old jovial self again. Laughing helped lift our spirits.

"Even after a semester of Driver's Ed, I can't drive either, so go for it," Kyra giggled.

The car was old, but was an electric hybrid, which present-ed me with one less problem of having to refuel at the NWC Sewage Waste Station, where we could be spotted. And it was fully charged. I pulled off the driveway with ease and drove as confident as I could so as not to attract attention to our age, our identity, or our lack of driving ability.

"Got any idea how to get to Wiskonset Parkway?" I asked.

"Wiskonset Parkway! That's been closed off to the public for years now, since the zoning changed for expanded Biosphere ac-tivities." Kyra paused and stared out the window, chewing her fingernails. "My dad...he used to take us out there for picnics. It was beautiful by the river. Now, well now, it's a Biosphere restricted area." Kyra paused and then looked a bit upset. "That's where we're going?"

"That's where my dad is," I replied, "maybe my mom, maybe Tommy, maybe even Mrs. Woodrow."

"Your Dad! This is pretty dangerous, Ang" Then Kyra grabbed my arm and yelled, "Ang, Ang! Turn Right! Right here! NOW!" I made a hard turn, careening inches from an old fire hydrant.

"Sorry Angie, but I noticed all those NWC police cars ahead. Not in our best interest to be traveling past them. Would pose a question or two."

Kyra was right. So, we traveled the busier streets to blend in with the heavier traffic. Small and seemingly abandoned streets would make us very obvious on surveillance cameras, which were everywhere. Too dangerous. I was already on the NWC hit list. Kyra might be as well.

"So, you found your dad and your mom?" Kyra asked puzzled. "When?"

"Oh, you wouldn't believe what I've been through these past few days. Way too much to explain right now. But for now, you need to know they're involved with the NWC and I have a mission that includes them."

"You know I never told you Angie, but my Dad... he did some things with the new world order too before he died. And he gave me some pointers on protecting myself."

"Your dad worked for them?" I asked surprised. "Why didn't you ever tell me?"

Kyra shrugged her shoulders. "There was really nothing I could talk about. And he didn't exactly work for the government. He was more or less contracted by them."

"So, he was a spy. You know they'll want your brain for their work. They might think they can control your mind like they controlled your Dad's mind. Maybe that's why they drugged you and spared your life for the time being."

"My Dad was a good man, Angie," said Kyra defensively.

"I'm not saying he wasn't. People do what they think they have to do for their families. But I bet he felt he had no choice," I replied. "Just how did your dad die, Kyra?"

"They found him on the side of the road. They said he had a heart attack and lost control of the car."

"Who said he had a heart attack? The NWC?" I asked, while checking the area to make sure we weren't being followed. Cameras were positioned at every corner along the way, with guard stations every two-hundred feet.

Kyra rubbed her forehead and let out a big sigh. "So my Dad probably came across some information that he wasn't authorized to know. Are you thinking he made a deal to keep me alive, Ang?"

"I'm thinking he might not be dead. Did you ever actually see his body?"

"N...no," Kyra stammered as she held back the tears. "His vehicle burned up. There were no remains."

"I kind of doubt that." I put my hand on hers. "We're going to find your dad, Kyra. The NWC doesn't care about deals or promises. They're deceitful, cut-throat killers. They do what they do with no conscience or remorse. And there's nothing, absolutely nothing, you can trust about them. They just might be keeping him around for his skills."

We rode for many blocks. The silence between us was as thick as fog. It seemed as if we were getting in over our heads. And if I didn't love Jesus, if I didn't know that God was in total control of this situation, of my life, of our lives, I would have turned back in total fear. It's hard to imagine people living without Christ.

"You know Kyra, my mission might seem overwhelming because there's so much to be done. But I know God has called me to do this. His angels are here to protect us. His will be done. Only

He knows the outcome. And Jesus... sweet Jesus will never leave us."

Kyra smiled. "So, tell me more about your mission, Ang."

"Oh, a lot has changed in my life, Kyra. I've been appointed to help make a real change in our world. And though I had moments of doubt, I now know the source of those doubts and that faith is the answer. I can see the presence of angels with their swords ready for battle. I've even felt the brush of angel's wings to assure my safe passage. I've seen their heavenly light and it calms my spirit. I know I'm never alone. I know I need not fear. I know God has blessed me with this calling."

"Now you're talking Angie," replied Kyra lovingly. "I always knew you were a chosen one."

"We're all chosen for something. You just have to believe, have faith, be patient and have hope, Kyra. It all seems mind-boggling, but it's not if you leave it all in His hands."

How beautiful everything was falling into place, I thought. *How beautifully laid out are God's plans. Even my dear friend was an important part of my mission, this mission. We all have our own gifts to contribute, all in His time.*

Kyra nodded in acknowledgement as she looked out the window. Out the corner of her eye she noticed what was going on behind them via the side-view mirror. She responded as calmly as she could muster. "Angie, don't look now, but we're being followed."

"Helicopters?" I asked.

"No, not yet. Ground surveillance, 4 x 4's, about 300 feet behind us," said Kyra nervously.

"Well, we've got to lose them." Dark shadows, hundreds of them formed a huge mist before me, filling the landscape as far as I could see. We were quickly being surrounded by the encroaching darkness. "Can you see them, Kyra! They're everywhere!" I tried to steer the car to avoid them.

"See what?" Kyra yelled puzzled.

I had no time to explain or to contemplate. "What do I do now, Lord?" I pleaded.

BELIEVE.

"What did you say, Kyra?"

"I didn't say anything."

BELIEVE.

The mists were coming ever closer to our vehicle. When I steered right, they trailed us to the right and when I steered left, they shadowed our car to the left, as if we were attached to a giant dark storm cloud of leviathan proportions. Fear was tempting me, trying to persuade me to go back home, to give up my journey.

BELIEVE.

Visions flashed through my mind...the chilling presence at the accident, the evil lurking the high school hallways, the shadows among abandoned buildings.

BELIEVE!

More visions flashed...my grandmom's tenderness, the soothing and welcoming light of the spirits of the clouds, the sign of the cross against the light of the moon, the protective charge of God's messengers.

BELIEVE!!...Faith is...

My strength was building, trust stampeding thoughts of retreat.

"I'm taking this road and driving alongside the river," I yelled to Kyra. "We can make this!"

"But you can't! It's all broken up and full of fallen rocks," Kyra cried, panicking. "The only way out is into the river! We can't go any further, Angie."

BELIEVE!!!... Faith is being sure of what we hope for and certain of what we do not see. [11]

"It's okay. I've got it. We have to keep going." My muscles relaxed as I swerved from right to left to avoid all the debris and fallen trees and the dark shadows that were trying to distract my focus. Just as I thought we were clear, another huge rock hit the tire axels and tipped the car sideways.

"Oh, no! Kyra! I can't control the car! Hold on! We're slipping off the cliff!"

CHAPTER TWENTY-FOUR

THE LORD'S HAND

"A righteous man may have many troubles, but the Lord delivers him from them all."
Psalm 34:19

I CAN ONLY DESCRIBE it as something like a plane ride, except for the part where we descended into the river. We flew for one hundred feet before gravity pulled Mrs. Woodrow's little red hybrid into a hard and heavy nose dive, into the cold waters below. With the front of the car deeply positioned in the river bottom, we tried desperately to open the windows to make our escape, but the pressure of the water was fighting us. It was only a matter of seconds before the car began to fill with water, momentarily leaving us with only a few inches of air space to breath.

"Kyra, help me kick out the front windshield." We both kicked as hard as we could. I grabbed the security club to try to break the glass, but the water cushioned the blows and lessened my strength, softening the impact. With no airspace left to breath, I didn't know what would happen next. Then outside the driver's side window, a huge twenty-foot long catfish appeared and was swimming in a circle around the car. I didn't know if it was there to help or if we were food. It swam closer and closer to my side of the vehicle.

Just as I moved over to Kyra's side of the car, the catfish spun itself with such force that its tail broke the driver's side window, giving us enough space to swim out. By this time, I was beginning to feel woozy from lack of air, but I mustered up enough energy to grab Kyra's arm, pulling her already limp and unconscious body toward me. I wanted to give her a breath of air, but I had none. I couldn't fight any longer as I myself began to lose consciousness. Then I felt a tug on my clothes and realized I was being dragged along the bottom of the river. The catfish had us both tightly clenched between its' jaws. In my delirium, I thought about Jonah in the belly of the whale. Just then the giant creature lifted us, higher and higher, out of the depths of the river to the surface of the water, where I drew in a life-saving breath, while being carried to dry land.

The giant catfish pushed us up onto the shores of the riverbank, then looked out the side of one eye and quickly descended to his home at the bottom of the river. He had carried us directly across from the 150 foot plateau sign that grandfather had mentioned. That would mean that we were at the base of the hill that housed Biosphere Six. I gave Kyra CPR until she began to cough out the water that had flooded her lungs. She slowly regained consciousness. I checked the other side of the Wiskonset for the 4 x 4 that had been following us, but they must have given up and traveled on. I looked around us and noticed a suspicious breach in Biosphere security, a convenient hole in the tall barbed wire fence surrounding the complex, allowing us easy access to the isolated fortification.

"What just happened?" Kyra asked as she lay staring at me. "How did we get on land?"

"A catfish rescued us," I mumbled.

Kyra squinted her eyes and with a half-smile asked, "A catfish? You bumped your head when we hit the river bottom, didn't you?"

"No! And it was a catfish, a giant catfish, like the giant whale that ate Jonah and spit him out when God commanded." Kyra was giving me that look of hers, like when I should know better. "It's in the Bible! And I guess no one believed the first guy who was saved from the sharks BY DOLPHINS AT SEA EITHER !"

"Alright, you've got a point there." Kyra paused and grimaced a bit.

"You know, help from God isn't always in human form. He

made all creatures."

"Okay! I believe you."

I took a deep breath. "Sorry. I'm just a bit agitated. Are you okay to climb now before we're noticed, because we need to move up into those bushes and hide for a while until dark. Less chance to be detected by surveillance." I pointed to the thickly wooded area up the hill.

"I'm fine," Kyra said and then hit me on the shoulder really hard. "But don't you ever drive off a cliff again! God doesn't want you driving off cliffs!" She was yelling at me but couldn't contain her smile, mumbling as we scaled the hillside.

We chose a thick cluster of mulberry bushes as our convenient refuge. Hunger was setting in and I remembered I hadn't eaten since Tommy and I had dined on Maria's vegetarian delectables at Mission City.

"Great time to be starving," I said.

Kyra reached in her pocket and pulled out four packages of cheese and peanut butter crackers. She shrugged her shoulders and smiled. "Hey, Mrs. Woodrow told me to help myself."

"You're a lifesaver," I whispered and patted her shoulder.

We carefully opened the packages under our shirts to muffle the sound. The aroma of the peanut butter attracted an unlikely sight...three curious squirrels.

"I remember these little guys when I was about eight years old," I whispered. "Nana and I used to feed them shelled peanuts."

"I thought they all died off from the chemical spraying," said Kyra quietly, "but I guess the NWC saved a few. They're so cute."

"The NWC wouldn't spray their own biospheres. They're not trying to kill themselves." We looked at each other and laughed as we shared half of our snacks with our little friends and then rested until it was dark enough to begin our climb to the top. Inching our way up, we braced our bodies against the steep slope, digging the toes of our shoes into the hardened clay dirt, and grabbing the thick strong foliage that laced the hill. Keeping inconspicuous amidst all the greenery, we gazed over the steep incline to take in the sight of the biosphere before us. I'd imagined a type of country living out here. I'd imagined spacious homes and apartments, shopping malls, clean working environments, progressive schools offering the best education, the best of the best resources. I'd imagined a life of splendor compared to the other zones. I thought there would be birds chirping, trickling brooks full of fish and people enjoying picnics. I'd imagined laughter and purpose. I thought that the people who were brought here were well taken care of in order to procreate and provide for future generations for this earth. But all I saw was one massive, hexagonal-shaped steel plate on the grounds, approximately four-hundred feet in diameter with a jet and two helicopters parked along its perimeter. Four manned security towers overlooked the area. There were no windows, no doors. Nothing.

"I don't get it," I whispered, turning to Kyra. "There's no building out here."

"Don't be so sure," Kyra whispered back to me, pointing at the unusual sight unfolding in front of us. The massive, six-sided plate rose slowly, arrogant in its ascent, as if peering in judgment at the surrounding countryside, until it became the roof of a four story, slate paneled, impenetrable secret hamlet. There sat the Biosphere complex, a good 300 feet from the summit of the 80 degree slope where we perched.

"My grandfather was right," I said. "He told me it would be close to impossible to break in. I can't quite figure this, Kyra."

Just then a slate door opened at ground level and a soldier emerged. He placed his right hand on his left shoulder and once again the door became an invisible part of the outer wall.

"Perhaps there's our entrance," said Kyra. "But how do we get in? He used some sort of device on his arm or something."

I shook my head. "We'll be okay, Kyra." I whispered. "I haven't a clue how to enter this place but we will. Ever since the accident, life has been just one big strange set of circumstances requiring never ending leaps of faith. We'll get in." I looked up and closed my eyes. "Heavenly Father, we need some help here!"

Kyra nodded in acknowledgement but looked a bit confused. "What were you saying about an accident?"

"Yes, the accident. I saw you there but with the ambulance and all the crowds of people, I couldn't get through to talk to you."

"I don't remember any accident. Whoa... Angie!" Kyra put out her hand to grab me. My legs had started to shake and I was beginning to slip on a thick pile of wet leaves. I reached for anything to grab hold of, to keep from slipping back down the steep hill. But the harder I tried to pull myself up, the further down I slipped. I strained to hold onto something, anything at all, but the bottom of the hill was getting closer. My arms were tiring. My struggle to stabilize myself was becoming more and more difficult. As I reached for a rock, I ripped open the side of my hand and blood began pouring out. A noxious odor surrounded us and I felt a presence but I could see no movement in the dark woods. The smell of my blood was attracting the guard dogs to our location. Surveillance lights brightened, scanning the hill that we clung to. Before I could stop myself from once again falling down the incline, I felt a foot on my back. Instantly we were surrounded by an army of stone cold, grey uniformed officers, pointing assault weapons at our heads. Above us, a helicopter zoomed in to our location and announced - "You have committed a New World Court offense. If you move, you will be killed." Metal stairs unfolded from the NWC37 surveillance copter. Uniformed security with heavy artillery, slid down the metal rails of the stairs and apprehended both of us.

"Angeleigh St. James and Kyra Christian, you are under New World Court arrest."

Our wrists were severely wrapped behind us and attached to a cable, which painfully lifted us up into the prisoner compartment of the armed helicopter. My muscles felt like they were being ripped from the bone.

"Where are you taking us?" I yelled. "This is one way to get in," I mumbled to Kyra.

"You have no rights. You have no voice," announced a guard

staring across from us. He raised his rifle and all else went black.

CHAPTER TWENTY-FIVE

SHADES OF DARKNESS

"The Lord will guide you always; He will satisfy your needs in a sun-scorched land and will strengthen your frame." Isaiah 58:11

I REGAINED CONSCIOUSNESS ON the floor of a sickly lit, six by four-foot cell. My head was pounding from the large bump given by the brutal NWC police. I rubbed my eyes to clear them and noticed I was at the end of a long, dark corridor. I remembered I'd been dreaming, a very strange dream where I was lying in a hospital bed. I don't know how I got there but IV's, electrodes and monitors were keeping me stabilized. My ribs were apparently broken and wrapped tightly. Surrounding my bedside stood all my friends and family. Some appeared as in a fog, almost spirit like. Mrs. Maple and Lady Maggie were there. Tommy, Kyra, Mom and Dad and my grandmom watched prayerfully. Behind them all, I could see Love and Faith and all the cloud spirits. For some reason, I couldn't talk to anyone. Then I woke to my dismal surroundings with dark shadows creeping around the corners of the cell walls. Keeping them at bay was a light glow that I knew was my angelic safeguard. The floor was cold and damp.

I thought of Kyra and I wondered where they had taken her. I spoke her name, hoping she would answer from the next cell. But there was silence.

"Is anyone there?" I called. "Is anyone out there?" But there was no response.

Oh Lord, how will you get me out of this one? I thought.

Then in the corner of my cell I noticed a figure, sitting comfortably on the floor. The glow from my protectors cast a gentle light on the face of the mysterious someone. I was getting used to all these strange occurrences, actually looking forward to experiencing God's next beatific provision. I rose to my feet and walked closer with little apprehension. It was...it was Lady Maggie!

"What are you doing here my friend?" I asked, concerned that she might also have been picked up for some serious offense by the NWC police.

She held out her hand and offered me a metallic, eight-sided object. It looked like a missing puzzle piece.

"What is this, Lady Maggie?" Having never heard her voice, I didn't expect her to answer. I analyzed the smooth-edged object closely. On one side, was an engraving of the NWC insignia, on the other, a number six. *Perhaps it was a type of coin, an emblem or a key of some sort,* I thought.

"You will need this for your mission," she quietly said to me.

Lady Maggie had spoken! Her voice was clear and pure and soothing. It was a calming voice, much like the beautiful voice of my Nana. It was a voice I needed to hear right about now. I sat on the cold floor and examined the eight-sided object again. "Lady Maggie, what purpose does this curious object have?"

Just then we heard the sound of footsteps in the distant corridors. "You will need this at the appointed time," she repeated as her body began to fade, becoming part of the exquisite luminescent glow of my protectors. *"Do not forget to entertain strangers, for by so doing some people have entertained angels without knowing it,"*[12] And Lady Maggie became part of the light. I remembered the Scripture as Hebrews 13:2, and a beautiful warmth tingled in my head and moved to my neck and spine, then circled my heart, and traveled to my arms and then my legs, and I felt in peaceful harmony with the spirit within me. I had no fear. Just as I hid the object in the secret pocket of my pants, the footsteps stopped outside my cell. Two guards unlocked the door.

"Up!" they demanded as they grabbed me, pulling me out of the cell and dragging me down the dingy hall. I made a mental note of my surroundings, paying attention to the exit signs. I assumed this was the basement of the biosphere, a very outdated looking basement. The floors were rough cement like those dungeons described in medieval novels. The hall's dull lighting came from the widely scattered oil-filled hurricane lamps hanging from the center beam of the cathedral high ceiling. There were no windows, no air ducts, only dampness and darkness and cold, clammy iron barred cells. I saw one set of stairs and an elevator. *This might be my escape route,* I thought.

We passed many cells with prisoners who were peculiarly quiet. They never looked up when as we walked by. All were laying still in fetal positions on their cots. I doubt if they knew if it was day or night, spring or fall, or for that matter, if the world outside even existed. Or did they believe they were the only ones left to suffer in this unknown underground concentration camp. As I passed all these lost and lonely souls imprisoned here, I prayed II Thessalonians 3:5, *"May the Lord direct your hearts into God's love and Christ's perseverance."*[13]. The movement on the walls was bizarrely familiar, the very same I sensed in the catacombs on our way to Mission City. Those same dark shadows were all around me, following my every move. I watched as they slithered along the walls and ceilings and around corners. I now believe the world is infested with these ungodly creatures. The unbelieving can't see them or feel them, nor did the unbelieving understand their own vulnerability. They don't know how necessary it is for them to come to Christ, their only protection.

The guards stopped as we approached the elevator. I turned to look at one guard behind me. His eyes didn't blink, his expression was void of emotion. There wasn't a hair out of place, nor a wrinkle in his clothes. He was like a breathing mannequin with exceptional strength. As the doors of the elevator opened, they pushed me in. I looked above the door and saw that we were leaving Sub-Basement 3, and that this building had six sub-basement levels and four above-ground levels, named A through D, the last being the ground floor. We traveled to Floor A. The doors opened to a large hallway with cold, unkept looking offices.

Bare concrete floors matched the bare concrete walls, accentuating its lackluster, with low-light fixtures, creating this medium for wickedness. Many exam rooms lined the hallway. One room with large picture windows particularly drew my attention. Inside, was what appeared to be five-foot long sharks swimming above the level of the floor in a waterless lab named 'The Hover-Land Shark Experiment'.

"One of your devious hobbies?" I remarked sarcastically, sneering at the nasty guards as they dragged me through the halls.

"Clones from the 2080's, used for border patrols," one guard replied bluntly. "Not your concern!"

The guards took me to the end of the long hallway where a sign indicated I was entering the main office.

"General, your prisoner. Sit!" the guard said sternly as he threw me into a chair. I looked around the room. Light visions were directly behind me, to my right and to my left. Being the only believer, I knew only I could see them in this room full of soul-less creatures. They were only visible to those who believe. They were keeping me safe and fearless, and keeping me focused on God's directives. *For all who believe, His love and mercy is truly sufficient. And His truth is not complicated,* I told myself.

In front of me, a man discussed business with three others. As he finished his conversation, he turned slowly toward me. The dim lighting emphasized his cynical, loveless, evil expression. There was no soul behind his stare. But his features resembled those of my father.

"You made it here much quicker than I'd expected," he said.

"You're not my father! What have you done with him! And what have you done with my friends!" My body shook with anger. I stood up just long enough to be pushed backed down into my chair.

"Gentlemen, Gentlemen, no need for violence. This little lady can't escape." He waved his hand. "Leave, I want to talk to her alone."

The men nodded. "We'll be guarding the door, Boss." I heard the door slam behind them.

"You're not my father!" I screamed angrily.

"Well, of course I'm not, dear. I am," his lips pursed and he tilted his head to the side, "his best parts." Then he laughed, waving his hand as if he was the master of creation. "Or should I say his worst?"

His cynical smile was nauseating me.

"Your father...possessed excellent leadership skills, and actually was one of the best in the areas of acquisition, domination and terror. All those bad attributes are what makes our world a better place."

"Better for whom?" I asked.

"Better, my dear, for the world I plan to create."

"You can't create what God has already created!" I proclaimed, affirming his blasphemy.

"Of course not, my dear. That's why I have to destroy it first. Little by little until..."

"Only the biospheres remain," I replied in disgust.

"Excellent! Excellent!" remarked the insolent general. "You certainly share the negative mind-set of your father."

"You don't know me and you don't know anything about my father. He is a good and godly man."

"Oh, he is, is he? Then why was he one of our soldiers, young lady?"

"You're lying! He could never be a part of this horrendous system!"

"Now you see, that's why you're here," said the general as he left the back of his desk and approached me. "You appreciate the time and effort I've taken to build this new 'horrendous system', as you call it. Very insightful description. So, let me get right to the matter at hand." He leaned toward me, looking straight into my eyes. I didn't flinch but looked directly at the monster before me.

"We need you...well," he laughed cynically, "we need parts of you." The general walked to his desk and turned on the intercom. "Gentlemen, take this repulsive creature out of here."

I felt rage escalating inside me, my blood pressure rising making my head feel like it would burst, my stomach burning from the excess acid hitting its lining.

"As much as I'd like the cloning process to give you extreme discomfort, my dear Angeleigh, I'm sorry to say you won't feel a thing."

"Cloning? That's how you plan to conquer God's earth?" I laughed boldly. "Your plans can never succeed. No matter what you think, God is ultimately in charge of all this."

"Look around you, little Miss." The evil general circled me and then patted my shoulder from behind, whispering in my ear. "Who's in charge...*HERE!*"

The guards entered the office, and as they picked me up out of the chair and escorted me out, I shouted, "You can't hurt my family and friends!"

"They are of no consequence, nor are you," replied the general nonchalantly. "But we shall have much to talk about when your valuable prototype releases all your memories to me... Ha, ha...ha, ha, ha."

I could hear his laughter grow louder as the door slammed behind me. I was taken by elevator two floors below, directly to the cloning lab - a sterile, metallic, cold-as-ice, horror chamber of sorts, attended by a grey complexioned, emotionless assistant, obviously another victim, stripped of his humanity and restructured under this new regime. I prayed, "This can't happen, Lord. I know my mission far exceeds my demise."

"Secure her in that chair, gentlemen," said the assistant. Restraints were applied as a nurse inserted a syringe into a vial of slime green colored anesthetic. She turned to me and prepped my neck, placing the needle firmly, ready to inject.

"I need you now, Lord," I petitioned silently.

CHAPTER TWENTY-SIX

OBEDIENCE

"Great peace have they who love Your law, and nothing can make them stumble." Psalm 119:165

"General, what shall we do with this?" He and his four bodyguards contemplated while looking at the cage where inside Tommy sat bound by duct tape.

"He's a tough one," sneered the general.

"Well, we can't clone him," laughed one guard.

"That ain't no joke. No bad can come from him, so what's the use," said another guard.

"What I don't understand," remarked the general, "is why doesn't he just return to his commander. He's worthless here. You can't pit a boy against a giant like the NWC. What can he do to us!"

"Guess he's just a diehard, General. And people believe in this!" commented a guard.

"Not for long!" replied the general as the five walked away in a bolt of laughter.

Tommy loosened himself from the tightly bound tape and rose to his knees and with hands folded in a position of prayer, he petitioned the Great I Am. "Father in heaven, I need an army, for

You know what's on the horizon."

CHAPTER TWENTY-SEVEN

DELIVERANCE

"I will save you; you will not fall by the sword but will escape with your life, because you trust in Me, declares the Lord." Jeremiah 39:18

THE CELL DOORS UNLOCKED on sub-basement level six.

"Not you, Thriambeuo. Everybody else, we're forming two lines as I call your name." The guard began calling off the names on his roster, directing the victims to stand in either the left or right lines. He then approached those prisoners on the left and touched their foreheads with a liquid from the vial clearly marked Formula DCT, rendering each one docile and defenseless.

"People on the left, follow Mr. Slayman. You are scheduled for security risk extermination," said the guard with no remorse whatsoever. "And the lucky people on the right, well, we've found a reason for you to live as part of our biosphere staff. Follow Mr. Killmanski for your initiation treatments." The guard pushed the switch to relock all the cells and turned to Michael T. "We'll be back for you soon. However, not soon enough as far as I'm concerned."

Michael paid the guard's remarks no mind. He was back in New World Court custody and he was mad. They had trashed his headquarters and apprehended his daughter. He knew this time the government had plans of extermination after they finished their cloning extractions on him. But he was determined not to be weakened by their experiments. He knew God had called him to a greater purpose and that he would be given a means to escape just as he had been given in the past. The government thought they were in control because he was once a soldier. He had in effect infiltrated their system and become a part of their military unit to gain information and in doing so, had successfully escaped with valuable insight into their operations. Now with this imprisonment, his mission was being delayed. At first, anger had consumed him. He'd punched holes in the walls, tore the sink from its fixtures, and pulled his cot up from its bolts in the concrete floor. He couldn't stop what had happened to so many of his soldiers at Mission City. He had failed. "What good is my strength if I can't protect those You've entrusted to me, Lord!" He closed his eyes, folded his hands in supplication and replaced his anger with prayer. He questioned his leadership abilities. He questioned his commission of guardianship. He felt nauseous at the thought that they might be hurting his one and only daughter. Releasing his discouragement to the Lord and laying his head in his hands, he pleaded, "Oh Father in heaven, what have I done?"

"Your very best," said a guard approaching his cell door.

Michael looked the other way. He couldn't acknowledge the arrogance of these ungodly creatures.

"Come Michael, your daughter needs you," said the guard as he unlocked the cell door.

"What?" Michael T stood up and studied the man's face. "You're not a guard are you?"

"Oh, I'm a guard alright. Just waiting for a chance to set things straight. This new government presents a tough battle, but then it's all a spiritual war for the soul, isn't it Michael?" The guard handed Michael T a NWC jumpsuit, complete with identification insignia. "You best wear this, less questions from the staff." Michael grabbed the jumpsuit, unfolding it. "So, not your first time here, is it," the guard said presumptuously.

"No. I escaped once," Michael said with some apprehension as he stepped into the suit, fitting it over his clothes. He couldn't quite figure this guard's intentions. He had grown to truly trust no one but Jesus. "The NWC copied my DNA samples before I made it out."

"Ergo the General," retorted the guard.

"Exactly," Michael T nodded.

"I'm Calvin Heartley, by the way." The guard extended his hand. "It's an honor, Sir."

"Hmm, a flesh-and-blood guard. You're one of the exceptions," Michael remarked.

"About five percent of us are un-cloned," replied Calvin. We're subjected to rigorous tests of allegiance and programmability. I managed to get all the answers right," smirked Calvin. "But then you know about all the testing and torture that goes on here. So, back to the matters at hand, we have a lot to do. Before you reunite with Angeleigh, we must pick up a friend of yours."

"Friend?" Still curious of the man's knowledge, Michael asked, "How do you know so much about me?"

"Oh, I've followed your work for years, Sir. Brilliant!" Calvin replied with high regard. "But now a young man named Tommy is waiting for us."

They moved swiftly via the stairs to the interrogation rooms on Level 5 where Tommy sat peacefully caged. Approaching his jail cell, Tommy mused, "They don't know who they're messing with, do they!"

"Apparently not! Why didn't you just break yourself loose?" Michael asked.

"I was waiting for you! According to His plans, you know," Tommy replied as they unlocked him from his cramped imprisonment. "Besides, it's all about the journey."

"Well, it's good to see you in one piece, old pal," Michael said, embracing his little friend. "By the way, this is Lieutenant Calvin Heartley. He's on our side."

"Yes, I know. Calvin and I go way back," replied Tommy acknowledging his friend with a handshake.

"Okay, we have much to do," said Michael as he turned to Calvin. "So, where's Angeleigh?" And what about Elizabeth?"

"Angeleigh is six flights up, my man," Calvin replied. "But Elizabeth, I believe we'll find her in the general's private quarters on Floor A."

"Well, let's get on with this," Michael T ordered as he held out his hand for Calvin to lead the way. "After you."

"Keep your hands behind you Tommy, for the sake of the corridor scanners. You know, appear as a prisoner." Calvin pulled out his ScanLock, a device the size of the average thumb with infrared sensors. "This will help us. It shuts down the scanners and each click gives us fifteen seconds of clear time. The general invented it. We use it when government procedures aren't followed according to protocol, what the general refers to as his 'undocumented sessions.' One can't expect integrity among deception," Calvin laughed and looked at his watch. "But now it's time to gather your flock. Our scheduled departure out of here is at 2300 hours via the general's mini-jet. Let's get to it, my Christian friends!"

CHAPTER TWENTY-EIGHT

FOREVER WATCHFUL

*"The Lord is good, a refuge in times of trouble. He cares
for those who trust in Him..."*
Nahum 1:7

"SHE'S GETTING OUT OF her restraints!" yelled the medical resident. "Are you ready to inject the correct dose of Sedatin, Nurse?"

"Stop," instructed Michael T as he, Calvin and Tommy stormed the examination room. "Drop the needle and move away from her!"

"General?"

Michael T grabbed the doctor from behind. "I feel rather insulted but this whole cloning process does have its perks, hmm?" Michael looked at Calvin and winked. "Me, seeming to be the general and all."

"Imposters!" yelled the bad doctor.

The nurse slowly reached for an emergency button below the storage shelf. Tommy intercepted her by impaling a scalpel into her hand, pinning her to the side of the cabinet.

"Hmm, clear blood." I noticed.

"That's how you know, Andy, no red blood, no oxygen. Only God's creations carry the precious oxygen that we all share by breath from our Father," remarked Tommy, weighing out his right hand, then his left, "clone or human."

"That and the chip in their neck," Calvin added as he unhooked Angeleigh from the exam table. Michael retrieved the sedative syringe and used it on the bad doctor, causing him to cave to the floor, unconscious. As Nurse Loveless was about to scream for help, Michael T threw a staggering left hook to her jaw. She fell to the floor, with her hand still pinned to the cabinet, the scalpel tearing at her cloned flesh.

Michael embraced his daughter. "Did they hurt you?"

"God wouldn't let them do that, Dad. Nothing can jeopardize my mission."

"You're after my own heart," said Michael T.

"Angeleigh, meet Lieutenant Calvin Heartley. He's here to help."

"Good to meet you, Lieutenant Heartley. Another one of God's helpers, I assume." *God is always faithful to his promises.* I thought.

Calvin nodded his head and remarked, "We're good then. Just up a few flights to Elizabeth and your family will once again be together."

"Dad, they've got Kyra too."

"I'm sorry, young lady," Calvin looked down to the ground, shaking his head. "Kyra Christian was taken to an undisclosed location for special processing, not more than an hour ago."

Michael T cupped his sweet daughter's face in his palms. "Angeleigh, we'll rescue your friend, but we must first ensure our own safe passage or we're no good to anyone."

"They've got my teacher too, Dad. Her name is Ann Woodrow."

"It will be hard enough to get the four of us out of here, Angeleigh."

"But Dad, she's my teacher and my friend." I looked down. "I can't leave her in this awful place."

Michael T paused. "Calvin, is Woodrow here?"

Calvin shook his head. "I don't believe so. The only intake cases in the past three days have been you, your daughter, Tommy and Kyra. But perhaps she's one of the general's top secret victims, one of his own little experiments. Let's check his private cloning suite on Floor A, the same place where we'll find Elizabeth."

Michael motioned for everyone to be on the move, smiling at the thought of once again seeing the gentle face of his beloved wife.

CHAPTER TWENTY-NINE

LIBERTY

"The Lord sets prisoners free." Psalm 46:7

MRS. WOODROW LAY GROGGY on the operating table. An IV saline solution flowed through her veins keeping her system stable in case of sudden shock. She had particular abilities important for acquisition. Beyond that, the NWC's only concern was to maintain stability until trait and element extraction was completed. Adjacent to her and connected via tubes inserted in their spinal columns, lay a generic dummy ready for transfer. Between them sat a Restructured Magnetic Resonance Imaging machine. RMRIs, as they were called. These were electronically altered re-inventions of the imaging machines of the early 1970's. Once used to detect body malfunctions on a cellular level, they now had the capability of transferring DNA blueprints to a Reconstruction Image Cloning Instrument, known as a RICI. Through its complex series of operations, any and all physical and mental properties, including and not restricted to physical appearances, skills, stored memory, diseases and health abnormalities, could all be transferred to the generic counterpart. Scientists were still not able to perfect the process to capture individual potential. That was a gift that could be given only by God Himself to each of His children. Nor were scientists able to truly duplicate the life giving properties of blood. Only Jesus could accomplish such magnificence. However impious, genetic engineering had reached dangerous new heights and was fast becoming the preferred method of choice for the NWC to populate the earth with their select clone counterparts.

"Alright, Mrs. Woodrow," said Nurse Goodman, "do you see the screen above you?"

"Yes," Mrs. Woodrow replied with the robotic mannerism that accompanies Formula DCT applications.

"Has she been given the proper dosage of Sedatin to render her useless?" complained Dr. Mortimus as he entered the lab, as if the whole world was his stage. Even as Chief Physician of the Cloning Department and Physician General of the NWC Administration - East Division, his arrogance far exceeded his rank.

"Yes, Dr. Mortimus, DCT and Sedatin. She's been prepped, Sir!" replied Nurse Goodman, annoyed as always with the bad doctor's attitude.

"Alright then, her mind is lucid and vulnerable and her body temporarily paralyzed. We are ready to play." The doctor grabbed his clipboard, studying her dossier.

"Mrs. Woodrow, Charity Woodrow," the doctor waved his pen light above her eyes to test their reaction response. "Mrs. Woodrow, look at the screen above you. You will see a beautiful view of the ocean." A vivid cobalt blue light scanned and recorded her ocular patterns onto the RMRI's memory base.

"That's mean doctor," scolded Nurse Goodman.

"You should know the procedure by now," reprimanded the bad doctor. "The patient has to view the screen in order to record her identity and render her submissive via the hypnosis scan or else the cloning process will not be effective. Must I spell out the steps every time, Nurse Goodman!"

"No, Sir," the good nurse pronounced crisply and began walking away, mumbling. "Hmm, luring her with an fake ocean view, you're deceptively mean."

"What was that?" Doctor Mortimus retorted with raised eyebrows.

"I said you need to get her to look at the screen...Sir!"

"Alright." Doctor Mortimus huffed as he walked toward the control room. "Position yourself behind the protective screen, Nurse Goodman. I would hate to have two of you compassionate, goody-two-shoes around!" Mortimus began choosing his cloning options, comparing NWC prerequisites to his personal preferences. "Hmm," he pondered, "I think I'll pick – Master's Degree Educator knowledge storehouse - okay; body appearance minus ten pounds - okay; hair color changed to blue-black - okay; likes watching classic sports videos - okay. Let's add - attraction to dark haired cloning physicians – okay. And we are good to go."

Nurse Goodman looked at him and sneered. His presence always gave her a slight queasy feeling in her stomach.

"Inject the Dupliprep, *IF YOU DON'T MIND !*" the doctor demanded.

Nurse Goodman slipped the needle into the vial of phosphorescent blue liquid that aided the transfer of genetic material. She filled the syringe to 10cc's, pushed the injector to release any air, tapped it and positioned the syringe against Mrs. Woodrow's neck, injecting slowly to prevent pain from the thick serum.

"Are you finally finished, Nurse! I don't know why you care so much!" Mortimus gave a heavy sigh in disgust as the nurse walked behind the protective screen.

"Honestly, if I want to get things done today, I should do them all myself! *READY TO CLONE !*" Doctor Mortimus yelled as he hit the final button. In the adjacent RICI, DNA blueprints were transferred as the stolen innocent life of Mrs. Woodrow breathed into the generic. The angels wept at yet another cloning atrocity and the NWC could once again revel in their mockery. Just then Mrs. Woodrow's heart monitor sounded the alarm as she flat-lined.

"Her heart, Doctor!" Nurse Goodman yelled. "Her heart has stopped functioning." Mortimus quickly positioned the DHR over the patient's failing heart.

"Nurse...ready...*CHARGE!*" The Digital Heart Resuscitator sent volts through her frail chest. But the monitor read no response.

"Get on with this, my lunch is waiting. Nurse...*CHARGE!*" Again no response. "This is ridiculous. I have things to do. She's gone!"

"We need to try again, Doctor! I saw a slight activity on the screen." Nurse Goodman prepared to charge with or without the doctors' help.

"I said she's gone! We have the best parts." The doctor pushed the DHR back into the negative position and looked at his roster, drawing a line through her name. "Charity Woodrow, you're dead. Bag her," he yelled. "Now, who's next on the list?"

Nurse Goodman stood quietly in respect at Mrs. Woodrow's bedside.

"Stop dawdling, Nurse, and get rid of her." The doctor reviewed his scheduling clipboard. "I see we finally have the general's assistant, Elizabeth St. James, the privileged Elizabeth, hmm?" Mortimus' eyebrows turned up in a contemptuous slant. "I suppose we should be a bit careful with her. So just in case of error, get her traits on disk."

"That's against the law!" replied Nurse Goodman. "Unauthorized replication comes with strong consequences, Sir! I can't be a part of this."

"And who is going to tell? You?"

"Well, no doctor, but not much gets past NWC investigators when they make their weekly reports. They'll..."

"That's enough, Nurse Goodman. When will you realize you're not in charge! Now make a copy as per my directives and prepare

Miss St. James for cloning. My escargot is getting cold!

CHAPTER THIRTY

REST

*"Come to me, all you who are weary and burdened,
and I will give you rest." Matthew 11:28*

MEANWHILE...

Above ground between the Doomed and Zone B, the woman
had successfully traversed the complicated series of steps to make
her way to the surface of the world, to the safe zone. The harsh light
of the early morning sun hurt her eyes and burned her grey-tinged
skin. She hadn't surfaced from her underground home for seven
and a half months, knowing well the Impregnation Mandates of
the NWC Law Enforcement Team. Only Biosphere residents were
selectively allowed to reproduce. Now she was brazenly attempting
to search for a quart of pure NWC processed milk to nourish
her and her unborn baby. Her extra-large clothing concealed that
she was in the family way and would also allow room for the
flat-shaped milk container. She would ceaselessly search house de-
livery ports until she located an unattended supply of milk. Her
family had pleaded with her not to surface, insisting it was too
dangerous, that she would be spotted by the government police.
But in that her husband had been taken by the government on
false charges and she didn't want to risk the lives of her parents,

she took it upon herself to risk her and her baby's life for much needed nourishment. Her family had told her to go to Mission City instead, that they would offer her the best help. But she didn't want to travel through the dangerous catacombs. As she quietly moved her way past the back doors of the neighborhood homes, satellite monitor tracking devices quickly zoomed into her coordinates from their 42,000 mile orbiting status. She had been warned. She knew the near zero odds of making it back alive. Within five seconds, the woman and her precious unborn baby lay dead from pinpoint laser termination accuracy. Phase One helicopters were signaled and swept into position to deposit E714 spray on the dead body, quickly melting the flesh. Phase Two dilution sprays followed to force the toxic remains into the underground sewage near where her family awaited her return. She never felt pain. The angels had rescued the innocent souls of her and her precious baby, to bring them home to peace.

CHAPTER THIRTY-ONE

THE RESCUE

"Be self-controlled and alert." 1 Peter 5:8

SINCE THE AGE OF sixteen, Michael had been her soul mate. They'd been through much in their short time together, but always remained strong as one.

A few years after beginning his mission, Michael's project was expanding to the point that he required transportation, both aerial and ground in order to take on the growing capabilities of the NWC. His friends at Doomed #22 who were also engineers, agreed to take on the task of helping to build these vehicles with his specifications. He would be away for a month. When he confronted Lizbeth with his project, she made the decision to stay behind at the mission where she could get the rest she needed. She had been depressed ever since leaving her daughter with her mother, but felt it was a safer environment for her. Little did Michael know that she had other plans. Before Michael left, he made her a promise that when the project was complete, he would come back for her and they would take their mission on the road. When Michael returned in just three weeks, Lizbeth was gone. Word on the street had it that she had surfaced to obtain drugs from the black market to soothe her heartache and subsequently became addicted. Michael was heart-broken. In his search for her, he was told that people had seen him speaking to his Lizbeth, that he was dressed in his one-piece black jumpsuit with the NWC insignia on the pocket. He knew what had happened. But Lizbeth didn't. She wasn't aware that this was not the man she had fallen in love with. She wasn't aware that the general had cloned himself for this encounter. Nor was she aware that he had used some of Michael's DNA to appear as the love of her life. Michael was furious. The generic stood before her as her beloved Michael and told her he had come to rescue her from doom. He brought her back to good health and she believed she owed her life to him. Now, Elizabeth was next in line for duplication, with her life being spared to be used for other purposes.

Nurse Goodman positioned the RICI over Elizabeth's body. She adjusted the dials for prep and double checked her settings. She adjusted her body for comfort, checked her IV for the correct amount of drips per minute. Elizabeth would be well cared for by Nurse Goodman, who fortunately, had never lost her compassion for God's children in spite of her many hours of New World Court conditioning training. And she knew that nothing could go wrong with this cloning transfer. The good nurse knew that she herself was expendable, and she knew Elizabeth wasn't.

Doctor Mortimus sat relaxing at his desk with his usual pot of vanilla pecan cappuccino, gourmet chocolates, cheese, and shrimp appetizers, spread like an ancient Roman banquet. Nurse Goodman did her best not to notice him out the corner of her eye, though he sat in full view with his office window facing the cloning lab. He was a deplorable man, uncompassionate, deceitful. He followed NWC directives only if they were in his best interest, and used what resources were available to him for his own dishonest gains. He dreamed of being a full-fledged NWC operative in the field, "where the real action was," as he so coldly put it. As Chief Physician General of the Cloning Department and Physician General of the NWC Administration, he actually ordered the practice of outdated medical procedures because they inflicted more pain than more modern techniques. He truly enjoyed persecution and death.

"Are you comfortable, Elizabeth? This won't take long dear. Just a few pre-procedural tests to do to keep you safe and comfortable." Nurse Goodman gently smoothed her patient's hair away from her face.

"Will I feel any pain?" questioned Elizabeth in her drug induced slow and garbled speech.

"No ma'am, there's no..."

"Alright, I know she's the general's girlfriend," interrupted the bad doctor, "but we can make another one of her, or five or ten or fifteen more. What's the difference!" said Mortimus in his usual loathsome bedside manner. "This one's so subservient, you won't be able to tell who's real and who's a clone. So..." Mortimus approached the RICI and hit the repro button. "There, all done now. Get this cleaned up, Goodman."

Nurse Goodman sadly looked at Elizabeth, who would no doubt suffer some shock and brain function disorder from being rushed through the transfer. She looked to the ground in dismay and noticed out the corner of her eye some activity in the hallway. A smile came across her face as Michael T and his comrades infiltrated the lab and caught Dr. Mortimus by surprise.

"Doctor, there's been a change in schedule," said Michael T as he, Calvin, Tommy and I entered as the force of faith that we were. Michael T quickly eyed the labs surveillance monitors in the room, noting all of them to be conveniently inoperative.

"The scanners, Doctor," reprimanded Michael T.

"Yes, Sir... they...um, they need...uh... I meant to report it...it just slipped my mind," Mortimus said laughing nervously, his voice quivering. "What with all the work we've had lately...Sir, I'm sorry...General...uh, Sir."

Nurse Goodman attempted to hide her slight grin. It wasn't often that anyone was able to humble this evil monster.

Relieved that the scanners were dead, posing no immediate threat to their presence there, Michael motioned for Calvin to secure the door.

"As I was saying," Michael T continued, "there's been a change in schedule. I need Miss St. James back in my office...*NOW!*"

"Yes...Yes, of course Sir," said Mortimus as Nurse Goodman moved the RICI out of the way and helped Elizabeth into a wheelchair. A knock at the door interrupted their rescue.

Calvin opened the door, motioning for Tommy and I to stand behind it, as two of General Thomas' personal guards entered.

"Excuse me General, but we require the assistance of Lieutenant Calvin Heartley, Sir. Two of the prisoners are missing."

"And who are these prisoners, Private?"

"The two children, Sir...the teenage girl and the young boy from Zone B."

My father glanced at Tommy and I, hiding very still behind the door. Michael T looked at the doctor with a stare that told him this was not his business.

"Very well, Lieutenant. But may I have a word with you first." Michael pulled Lieutenant Heartley to the side and asked quietly, "How did these guards know to come to me instead of the real general? Is he not in his office?"

"Well, we couldn't risk the confusion," Calvin whispered. "I put his office intercom settings on 'conference'...a virtual do-not-disturb sign, so to speak. So let's just say that General Thomas is a bit disconnected from things right now." Calvin smiled with a very pleased look on his face.

Dad nodded and retorted, "Yes, Lieutenant, please go with these men. And Lieutenant Heartley, 2300 hours."

"Yes, Yes, of course, General." The officers saluted and escorted Calvin out the door.

Meanwhile Dr. Mortimus was looking suspiciously at the children. "What's going on here!" Mortimus asked apprehensively.

"What's going on here?" angered Michael T. "What's going on is that I have my own plans for these young lawbreakers. Is there a problem, people?"

"No General, not at all," replied Mortimus cautiously.

Nurse Goodman just grinned.

"And your roster, Nurse. Let me see it."

"Yes, Sir." She lowered her head as dad read the entries, noticing the words, 'Charity Woodrow-Deceased.'

My dad looked at me. I could see in his eyes what he had just learned. My sweet teacher had died at the hands of these monsters.

Dad grabbed mom's wheelchair, and motioned for us to walk in front of him, leaving the lab, all the while keeping an eye on Mortimus.

"And report these scanners to maintenance or you will be dealt with. Are you trying to hide something, Mortimus? Perhaps some shady procedures?"

"No Sir, sorry Sir! Always according to rules, Sir!"

Leaving the lab, I glanced back at Nurse Goodman and at the satisfied look on her face. I wasn't quite sure what was up with her, but so far she seemed to be on our side.

As my father closed the door behind us, he whispered to Tommy and I, "Children, we have nineteen minutes to meet our rescue copter. But first we must make a visit to the general's office and I must try to talk my wife through the drugs they've given her so she won't create any suspicions."

"Elizabeth, Elizabeth," Michael said softly as he kissed her lips. "We have a secret mission, Elizabeth. I need your help."

CHAPTER THIRTY-TWO

BEWARE

"Do not be deceived: God cannot be mocked." Gala-tians 6:7

"Hello General," Michael T said with contempt as he stared at the abomination of his own DNA.

"How did you get in here?" the general asked, reaching for his intercom. "Guards! Guards! My office, *NOW!*"

"That won't do any good, General. Seems there's been some schedule changes and you're in conference... with *ME!*"

The general again reached for his intercom.

"What don't you understand? Your guards have been given alternate orders," said Michael T in a thoroughly condescending tone. He had waited so many years for this confrontation.

"What are you talking about, Michael? No one can give orders *BUT ME!*" said the general pounding his desk as if to scare his intruders.

"You New World Court people are amazing," Michael T scoffed as he walked around the general. "No orders can truly be fulfilled but those of the Lord God Almighty Himself. But you wouldn't be familiar with my God, now would you."

"Oh, I'm familiar, but perhaps you and your little band of renegades haven't kept up with our new world, a world you have no place in, Michael," said the general with a venomous smile on his face, as he sat down at his desk, lighting a cigar. "Michael, Michael, you will never make it out of here. Why don't you give up before you get you and your precious little daughter killed? I just might let you live," said the general tilting his head in thought, "as my servants."

"You have no control over my life. And besides I've decided to invite you to my home, for say, a nice little stay of rest and relaxation."

General Thomas laughed at Michael's proposal. But Michael T wasn't laughing.

"Now, come with me General, we have a jet to catch, Yours!"

The general smiled. "You must be out of your..."

Michael threw a left hook to the general's solar plexus, making him gasp for air and then a right jab to his jaw, leaving him defenseless. The General fell to the floor unconscious.

"That felt good. He's been fighting me for a long time." Michael mumbled.

"What was that, Dad?"

"Nothing, nothing. I'll tell you another time." Michael stared at the general lying on the floor.

"When did they clone you, Dad?"

Dad sighed. "It's a long story. Too long for now. Alright people, let's dress the general in my street clothes," said Michael T as he began to remove his WC uniform.

"What is go...ing...on," mumbled Elizabeth. By now the sedative was wearing off. Elizabeth looked around at all of us, trying to focus her eyes, confused by her surroundings.

"Angeleigh, tend to your mother. And Tommy, help me redress the general." Tommy removed the general's attire as Michael switched from his jumpsuit into the general's dress uniform. Michael T fixed his cuffs and looked at Tommy and said, "Now, there should be no question in anyone's mind who I am or shall I say who I'm supposed to be."

Dad turned to me. "Angeleigh, how's Mom?" I'd never heard that question before. The words were so sweet that they brought tears to my eyes.

"Let me see, Dad." I placed my hands under her arms, straddling my legs around hers to guide her and give her support. "Mom, can you stand up? Push up on the arms of the wheelchair, Mom."

"Why do you call me mom, young lady? Who are you?" My mother looked deeply into my eyes, searching. Though she hadn't seen me in many years, I knew once the drugs wore off she would know in her heart that I was her daughter. I couldn't deal with her rejection again. I needed to see genuineness in her eyes. I needed to see true love for her child.

"Mom, I'm Angeleigh, your daughter." My heart was racing, troubled about what might be my mother's reaction. My eyes were fixed on hers. I didn't blink. I didn't breath. Every thought I had of my mother in my entire life passed through my mind. She searched my face as I searched hers. From my pictures of her, she had barely aged, but her eyes had lost the innocence of her youth. I would have recognized her in a crowd of thousands. But I wondered if she could see any essence of her little baby in me. I didn't want to know her answer, but I couldn't wait any longer. And then my lungs involuntarily took a deep breath and a calm came over my spirit. Again, I reminded myself that God hadn't brought me this far to be disappointed. And as the cloud spirits had said, my parents were to accompany me on my mission. Whether my mom accepted me or not, would never change God's plan. My father loved me, my nana loved me. I could wait for my mother to love me. I gently placed my mother's hand in mine and brushed back her hair from her forehead. My mother raised her eyes slowly and with a dead stare, yelled out, "You're not my daughter!" The room dimmed and a chill ran past me as dark shadows oozed from the walls, permeating my surroundings with their wicked and unforgettable stagnating odor. My father stood firm at their presence.

"Something's about to happen, Dad," I said nervously.

The woman that I thought was my mother stood up and reached for the laser rifle that was mounted on the general's wall.

"Angeleigh," my father warned me, "move away. This isn't your mother."

"You people are trespassing, and I am programmed to shoot you on site." The woman waved the rifle wildly between the three of us.

"Sorry, your programming days are over," announced Lieutenant Heartley, as he entered the room and applied the Clonex laser to her neck. Quickly, the woman's system was disabled and she fell to the floor. Calvin knelt down and cut a half inch opening at the base of her scull, removing a red microchip.

"It holds recovery and maintenance features," explained Calvin. "She's done. Sorry it had to come down like this. You can never be too sure who's a prototype and who's human."

"I'm not quite sure how she did it but somehow Nurse Goodman switched her when we raided the lab. Can't imagine why she'd do such a thing, unless she was trying to protect the real Elizabeth." Dad said, dragging the prototype to the corner of the room, where he brushed his hands clean.

Calvin walked over to the general, incapacitated on the floor and asked, "We're taking him?"

"I'm sure the NWC has an abundance of software on his duplication, so why bother. Just shut him down," replied my Dad, scratching his chin. "And Calvin, is it possible to access those replication files?"

"You mean these?" interjected Tommy, as he held out a small roll of media discs.

"My good friend, when did you pick these up?" asked Dad.

"When we were in the lab. Seems Dr. Mortimus is a little sloppy and leaves his own stash of illegal duplications out in the open. Saved us a few minutes of sorting through computer files!" Tommy grinned as he briefed through the names written on the sleeve of the tube. "Well, we've got Elizabeth, Mrs. Woodrow...a few others, most likely of particular importance to Dr. Mortimus, and here we go...Voila! The General!" Tommy smiled and then a troubling look came across his face. "Well this explains a lot."

"What's that?" asked Dad.

"Seems the higher-ups gave the general a code name," replied Tommy, "perhaps to represent a genetic aberration that was created during cloning. Basanistes. It's a Latin word found in Matthew 18:34 describing the conduct of a jailor. It means one who uses torture to obtain information."

Dad picked up the storage roll and flipped it in his hand. "This is no surprise. The New World Court has big plans for this guy. It's too bad it's not the master copy, but it will have to do." "When we get back to Mission City, we can learn more about their operations and hopefully halt some of their prototype procedures. We have to stop this madness." Dad shook his head and then looked at his watch. "Well Calvin, remove the general's chip and let's be on our way."

"What about the innocent people in the cells, Dad?"

"Angeleigh, we can't possibly conquer the entire system with one initial mission," replied my Dad. "Our plans were to take over this biosphere, but we lost manpower with the massacre. Now we have to go back to square one. We have a lot of rebuilding to do. In the meantime, we've got some vital software, much more information than we had before."

"Michael," said Calvin as he hacked into the general's mainframe, "give me a minute. Maybe we can't take down the biosphere just yet, but there's more data available to take with us." Calvin removed a micro disc from the general's top desk drawer and attached it to the base of his neck. "All Biosphere personnel are equipped with a mini-CPU, a sort of computer workstation, near the base of their brain," Calvin explained. "Among other more controlling uses like receiving direct orders, it also functions as an internal hard drive for file transmission and data functionality. When I attach this magnetic micro-disc to it, the information is transmitted via the micro-media drive through my synaptic brain matter to my optic nerve where it's reflected onto a sort of holographic screen which you see before you." In front of us materialized a giant electron display. "You're looking at the SPS or Station Position Status of the entire Biosphere system," explained Calvin. "It gives us a roster of guards, two hundred and ninety thousand to be exact, ten thousand per region, and their station positions by date. This roster covers all guards across the country and in fact the globe." Calvin exchanged the micro disc with a blank one and looked at the pixilated screen. "This system is thought, as well as voice activated. I think print to disc and the information is now copied onto the blank media. Pretty interesting," Calvin smiled. "We can use this disc in the future to commandeer our infiltrations better." Calvin removed the new disc from his neck and placed it in his uniform pocket as he continued his scan for guards on level 6. "Michael, I think we can free those men in the cells. Okay, there are currently seven guards on duty on level 6, of which there are three between the cells and the emergency exit. Only Level 6 is occupied with candidates for reprogramming, the rest of the prisoners in the dungeon appear to be exterminated." As he proceeded to open each guard file, I saw him enter: Deprogram and Deactivate. "They won't be a problem now. I'll set programming to raise the roof immediately. We'll be ready for take-off. But one more thing..." Calvin began searching through the general's desk drawers.

"What is it? What do you need?" Michael asked.

"A LaserLok device. It's small, metallic...has eight sides."

"Is this what you're looking for?" I asked.

Lieutenant Heartley looked at Tommy and I. "Well, you two

are full of surprises. Where'd you get this?" Calvin examined the device. "This is definitely not one of the newer models, but it will still do the job."

"Let's just say it was a gift from a friend." I replied.

"This will save many lives. We can set free all the innocent prisoners safely with this. Thank you, Angeleigh," Calvin said, waving the LaserLok.

"Why can't we deactivate everyone here?' I asked.

"We don't have that much time, Angeleigh," said my dad.

"Well, blow up the biosphere then," I retorted. "They're all clones anyway!"

"There are still some of us here that are dedicated to the 'good fight' or can be saved with deprogramming," said Nurse Goodman as she assisted the real Elizabeth into the room. "I'm sorry I didn't trust you all at first. I needed to be sure. When you left the lab I looked up Elizabeth's secret dossier and realized that you, Angeleigh, were Elizabeth's long lost daughter, and you, Michael T! Well, it's about time! What took you so long!"

"Nurse Sarah Goodman is one of us, Michael," replied Calvin, welcoming her presence.

Dad embraced his wife. "How I've missed you, Elizabeth. We will never part again," he said as he helped to steady her.

"We are going home family. Would you like to come along, Sarah?" asked Dad. "Mission City could use good people like yourself."

"I think I could be of better use to you here," Sarah smiled. "I'll do what it takes to help you take down this evil operation. Whatever you need, I'm here. But I'd better get back to the lab before I'm missed. Until next time," she waved as she left the room. "God bless you all."

"Alright, back to the matter at hand. We must move quickly," Calvin said as he turned to Michael. "I can release the prisoners through the river exits on ground level. When they escape, there will be a diversion so they can deploy into the fields. It's the best chance they'll all have to get away safely." Dad acknowledged Calvin's plan and shook his hand. Calvin saluted as he left the office. "I'll meet you on the roof at 2300 hours my Christian friends."

"God be with us all," replied my father. On the way out the room, my dad clicked on the Biosphere intercom, and announced, "Attention military officers of Biosphere Six: the following prisoners, Angeleigh St. James and Tommy Watchthee have been apprehended and will be escorted personally by yours truly, General Thomas, to Biosphere Seven for further interrogation. Elizabeth will accompany me. We anticipate take-off at 2300 hours. Prepare the mini-jet immediately. Over and out." My Dad clicked off the intercom, being very pleased with himself.

"Family, look," Dad said to me as he pointed to the vision above us.

"They're here to escort our safe trip home," I said reassuringly. My ever-present protectors hovered above us in brilliant illumination. They were our comfort and our direction. If only non-believers knew of the treasures they could have access to when they have faith in God. If only they would believe they are not alone in this world. If only they would give their hearts to the Lord, so they could follow the destiny that God has given each one of us. Then perhaps the people on this earth would know true peace. True peace, only to be found through Jesus. I felt so blessed to be given such a mission to encourage others to know the truth.

We were on our way home, I thought. But then things are not always as they seem.

CHAPTER THIRTY-THREE

SET FREE IN CHRIST

*"He brought them out of darkness and the deepest
gloom and broke away their chains."*
Psalm 107:14

CALVIN INTENDED TO TAKE the stairs straight to Level 6 but had
to detour on Level 5 due to some untimely building repairs. At
Level 5's station, six guards took it upon themselves to take a break.
As soon as they sighted Lieutenant Heartley, their conversation
ended and they dispersed to their respective posts.

"Gentlemen!" greeted Calvin.

"Lieutenant," remarked Private Dauntler in salute. "Good
news, they found the prisoners, Sir."

"Yes, I heard the announcement, Private. Now things can get
back to normal," replied Calvin. "But why are you all standing
around? Haven't you heard? There's a meeting with Colonel Dire
in a few minutes and he doesn't take to tardiness."

"Ah, yes Sir, Lieutenant." The three stood in attention nervously.

"By the way, who's scheduled for this post?"

"I am, Sir," replied Private Zitman.

"Well, carry on men." Calvin nodded, leaving the area with a slight smile. Everything according to plan, he mused to himself as he entered the elevator and pushed the down button, praying this one was operational.

The elevator screeched like worn-out brake shoes as it descended to Level 6. Deactivated guards littered the floor of the dungeon. Prisoners were yelling amongst themselves, while trying to shake open the cell doors. When they saw Calvin, the men settled down.

"People, listen closely," Calvin announced. "You are all to be free men, but you must strictly follow my orders."

"How can we believe him!" mumbled one prisoner.

"This is a trick!" yelled another as all the prisoners began yelling in fear and anger, banging the cell bars with their hands.

"Please! Quiet!" demanded Calvin. "I am here to help. I am here to release all of you."

The room became still as one prisoner asked with apprehension, "Alright, what do we have to do?"

"Horatio," said Calvin directing his orders, "I am putting you in charge of time synchronization. Men, I will guide you all to the exit point. Upon deactivating the exit security system, you will all then have exactly ninety seconds to evacuate and get past the boundaries of the compound." Calvin pushed the cell door release button. The men, young and old, gathered around him to quietly listen.

"What about the guards outside the building, Sir?" asked Horatio.

"I've taken care of all that," replied Calvin. "Your only concern will be to get past the invisible boundary walls and make your way down the steep outer hill to the river embankment, where heavenly messengers will guide you through the darkness. Do not be afraid. What is out there cannot hurt you. You are being protected. It will be treacherous, but you can all make it. Time is of the essence as is a quiet and safe journey. Now, let's all move to the emergency exit where I'll tell you more."

"Wait!" interrupted Horatio. "Many of us have brothers scheduled for security risk extermination. We believe they're still alive, Lieutenant Heartley."

"They must still be waiting in the dungeons," Calvin said, biting his lip as he thought. "Men, you wait here. We will bring the men back and then make our escape. Horatio, please come with me."

Calvin unlocked the heavy, iron gate that led to the hidden dungeons down below Level 6. A long dark stairwell and cold, damp corridor brought them to a cell packed with one hundred and seventeen men, standing room only and lit only by one oil lamp that hung on the wall outside the cell.

"Horatio!" a prisoner yelled out in desperation. The men began banging on the cold and rusty bars.

"We are here to take you to safety," instructed Calvin. "There is no time for questions. You must follow us quietly, men."

The stronger of the men helped those who suffered from the debilitating weakness and confusion that their daily DCT applications caused them. They traveled back up to Level 6, reuniting with the thirteen men there, and then struggled their way up five flights of back stairwells, where they finally arrived at their departure point.

"You have two minutes, people," Calvin addressed the men and then turned to Horatio. "I have programmed this door to open at the appointed time of departure. As you exit, hold this key before you and count sixty steps." Calvin handed him the eight-sided metal object that Angeleigh had received from Lady Maggie. "This is a LaserLok. It will turn a fluorescent green to indicate you may pass through safely without setting off deadly laser beams, as you approach the invisible boundary walls of Biosphere Six. Keep your hand extended and let the others pass before you, until they are safely through. You will have help that I cannot fully explain to you right now, but the believers in the group will understand what I am talking about. Then get to the river. And again, all this must be done in ninety seconds. I pray you will move quickly to get to safety. Do you all understand?"

"Yes, Lieutenant." The crowd responded.

"But why are you doing this?" asked one prisoner.

"Because..." Calvin paused, "because it must be done. I am just the messenger. Some of you believe in God, some don't. But I think we should all now join hands and bow our heads in prayer." Believers and unbelievers alike extended their hands to form a circle. Many of the unbeliever's hearts miraculously were touched by the Spirit this blessed moment as Calvin led the men in prayer.

"Father, be our guiding light and our strength, and deliver us from our transgressors. We come to you humbly in the name of our precious Lord, Jesus. Amen." All one hundred and thirty men responded with a strong "Amen."

"Men, once you make it to the river, you choose your destinations," said Calvin. "You may choose to return to your families. However, that will be the first place the NWC will look for you. If your heart so directs you and if you can get to the old Harbinger Warehouse in Zone B, you will be offered sanctuary for service to fight this system. Now I must go."

"But Lieutenant, come with us!" the men replied in unison.

"I can't go with you any further. Be ready when the door releases, Horatio! God be with you all."

The men thanked Calvin as he passed them and disappeared into the stairwell on his way for the final rendezvous on the roof of the compound.

CHAPTER THIRTY-FOUR

THE MISSION HAS JUST BEGUN

"...being confident of this, that He who began a good work in you will carry it on to completion until the day of Christ Jesus." Philippians 1:6

"STAY FOCUSED ANGELEIGH," MY father warned me. "Don't give in to their attempts to weaken your faith." Every inch of the hallway walls, ceilings and floors were alive with squirming dark shadows reaching out at us, pulling on us, trying to steal away the purpose that God had blessed us with. This time, they were massive shadows with a deafening hum accompanying their attack.

"They're mutating, Dad. Now they're moaning."

"Sounds like they're in pain, Angeleigh. Their hunger to steal our trust in God can't be fulfilled."

I turned and stared at them. "Accept your defeat because Jesus stands before us in every situation with His hands outstretched, telling us, 'Don't be afraid; just believe.'" [3] I spoke loudly over the assaulting noise. "We must focus and no harm will come to us." We all held hands and proceeded through the threatening thickness of death that surrounded our every step. But faith is a powerful sword that cleared our paths before us like the parting of the Red Sea.

"The closer you are to fulfilling God's will, the more you'll experience the resistance trying to discourage you," Dad said and pointed, "over there...we'll take those stairs to the roof...just one flight up." Doubt held out its ugly hand, but could not tempt us. The Light was stronger and reigned supreme. Darkness clung to the walls, shuttering at the heavenly bodies before them and then retreated into the darker cavities of their surroundings.

As my father reached for the door to the stairs, a cold hand grabbed him with a super-human grip.

"General," said the heavy voiced officer. "Pardon me, Sir, but we have a 245 Section 3 violation."

"Remove your hand from mine, Sergeant!" my father demanded. "Explain to me your insubordinate actions!"

"You know we can't make an exception when an officer has been deactivated and his chip is missing, Sir." The adamant Sergeant maintained a firm grip on Dad's hand. "We've found this violation on the General's counterpart. I'm afraid I must apprehend you temporarily."

"You dare question me, Sergeant! Do I look like one of the lowly clones to you! I am Basanistes!" My father's face was turning red from anger, an obvious reaction for a human but never to be associated with cloning material, nor with the real General Thomas who could deceptively remain undisturbed. The officers quickly pulled out their Bios-communicators, preparing to sound a high alert-security compromise code.

"Step back family," announced my father. No sooner did we move out of the way than my father made a backward flip, kicking both officers in the face. They fell to the floor and immediately rose again, like the evil they were, refusing to lose. As my father came down out of the air, he again kicked them on their backs, knocking them to the floor. Again they rose. In typical cyborg manner, they showed no signs of pain and resumed their offensive stance. My father's knowledge of New World Court battle protocol kicked in and he rose up into the air out of a standing position, kicking each one in the left side of the neck making their chips fully exposed. With the speed of light, my father extracted their maintenance chips and the officers collapsed, disabled.

My father took a breath. "No time to waste, family," said Dad as he led us up the stairwell leading to the roof. "We have no idea how many are aware of General Thomas' deactivation."

The vile essence of discouragement clung to the walls of the stairwell as if to make one last attempt to cause us to question our faith. Reaching the roof was no assurance that the shadows were left behind. Faith was our only sure and certain shield.

"*Faith – of greater worth than gold,*" [14] I proclaimed to our adversaries.

Along the four corners of the roof sat three helicopters and the general's mini-jet. Heavily armed guards maintained security. When we arrived, Calvin was waiting for us at the main entrance leading to the jet port.

"They know, Calvin. They know the general has been shut down," whispered Dad.

"Michael," he instructed, "There's a leak, but I think we're ahead of it. Stay calm. Right now, you are the general and we're following you out. Our angelic protectors will take us to the mini-jet docked at our two o'clock position. And very importantly," Calvin continued, "time is a critical factor here. As our jet takes off, 130 prisoners will make their escape from the rear exit of the building to the hill country. Even one second delay could cause them their death as well as deem us perpetrators. We must proceed in faith and confidence. Do we all agree?"

We all acknowledged his plan.

My dad turned to me and cradled my chin in his palm.

"Never forget this, Angeleigh, you'll know me by the blood."

My dad turned to face us all and said with a smile - "Ready family? Then, let's go with God!"

It was raining heavily, a strange cold rain, making the roof slick.

We walked swiftly, steadfastly following our heavenly escorts as they fully encompassed us. Guards watched us but didn't question.

"General Thomas," said a voice from behind us.

I looked at my father and he nodded to me as if to say, ' it's okay, don't worry'.

"Yes, private, what can I do for you?"

"May I speak to you a minute, Sir?"

"Of course," said my father with a rather suspicious look in his eyes. He checked his watch. There was only one minute, nine seconds to resolve this issue and make the scheduled departure. "Lieutenant Heartley, see to it that Elizabeth and the prisoners are secured tightly in their seats. I'll accompany you momentarily." We all boarded the mini-jet as my father stepped off with the officer. I tried to spot them through the window behind me, but they disappeared into the rain and fog. I looked nervously at the digital clock on the jet's operational panel. It now read 2259 hours and 31 seconds. Less than a half minute to go.

Calm down, I told myself. I knew once my father was in the jet, I would be able to rest easy that we were on our way home. But the sounds of firing rounds of ammunition interrupted my attempt to relax. NWC police rushed to a scuffle in the corner of the rooftop. "Stop them!" one man shouted. Then like the impending cataclysm of a level F5 tornado, where deep gloom approaches unnoticed and in the blink of an eye, buildings and sidewalk pavements are stripped away from neighborhoods, we were entombed in a sarcophagus of caustic, unearthly darkness.

The jet began to shake on all sides, trembling as if immersed in human terror, convulsing close to the point of being torn apart.

Tommy took my hand. "Relax," he said, "I've called on the armies of God to intervene." I looked at the jets digital departure timer. It read 2259 hours and 55 seconds. The doors locked automatically to prepare for take-off.

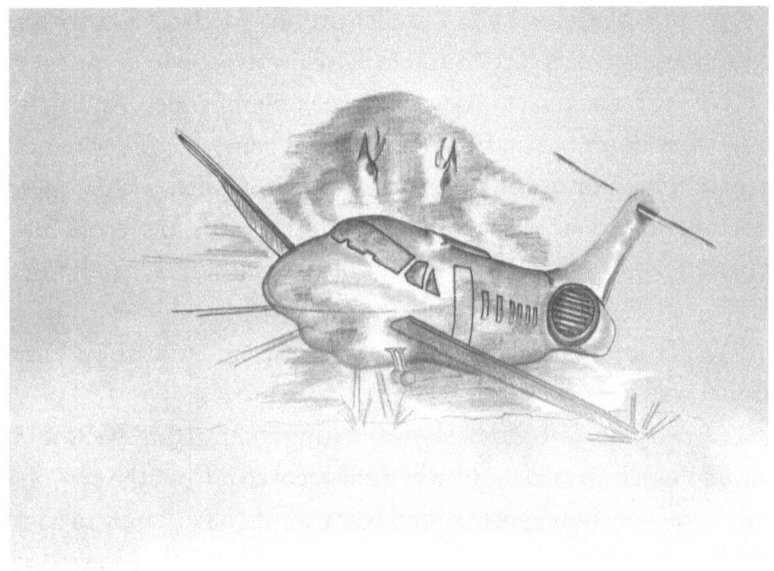

"My father's still out there! Open the doors, Calvin!" I yelled as I released my seat belt and made my way to the front of the cab in an effort to kick the doors open.

"Wait, Angeleigh. Have faith." yelled Calvin.

"*Faith is being sure of what we hope for and certain of what we do not see*", [11] I told myself.

The clock read 2259 hours and 57 seconds. The jet was shaking, shaking until I thought it would flip over. Outside there was pounding, furious and frenzied wrathful pounding. And then it stopped. And there was calm.

"It's Michael! Open up!" yelled a voice from the deep dark outer mist. "2300, Calvin," the voice said calmly. "2300."

Calvin looked at me. "*If God is for us who can be against us,*"[15] he said as he released the lock on the passenger side. In stepped my father.

"Go!" dad demanded.

Calvin put the jet into take-off mode and it ascended from the roof port as the gunfire ensued.

"We're safe, this vehicle is bullet-proof," Michael said with a temporary sigh of relief. "But they'll follow us, Calvin."

"Not without direct orders from their commander. And right now, they don't quite know who the real general is. They're not programmed for decision making," Calvin replied with a questionable grin, as he adjusted the navigational dials to prepare destination co-ordinates. "Straight to the old Harbinger Warehouse, Sir?"

"Yes, co-ordinates XI-B24. We can descend to Mission City from there."

I turned to look at Mom. She was resting comfortably. We would have so much to talk about when she recovered from the complications of her cloning procedure. Nana would be so happy to have her daughter back. *Thank you, Lord*, I prayed quietly. I looked at Tommy who appeared at ease beside me. Everything had gone well. We were going home and my parents and I were together again, but I still felt somewhat...empty. I contemplated the right words to express my feelings.

"Much good has come from this mission, Tommy," I paused. "But in all the good that's happened, I feel I've failed God. My mission was to encourage others to believe. I haven't done that. I haven't saved anyone. Only I've been saved from dangerous circumstances by God's mercy. I don't know that God is well pleased with me." I looked at my reflection in the jet window, unhappy with what I saw. "Why did God choose me for something so important?"

Tommy gently smiled. "Because He knew you were able. He made you to be able." Tommy grabbed my hand in his. "Andy, your faith has grown greatly and your mission has just begun. Know this, you must truly believe before you can spread the message of truth and hope to anyone else. Don't underestimate His power. God knows your heart and what He made you capable of. And you think you haven't encouraged anyone to believe? But you have."

Tommy pointed to the miraculous vision out the window. "See those men down there. Because of your mission, many have turned their life over to Christ Jesus. They are now truly set free."

I turned to look out the window at the biosphere's side exit. One hundred and thirty men made an invisible exodus, concealed by a heavenly multitude of angelic guardians. Only those blessed with belief in the wonders of God could view this miraculous vision. The grounds surrounding them were one massive gel of moving, wretched, consuming darkness, angry at the fact they would never be able to attain the peace that accompanies faith in God. The darkness made every attempt to infiltrate the angelic shield and pierce the hearts of the young converts within, but cringed and cowered at the sight of the heavenly company, as the Spirit of truth and righteousness caused it to draw back far from view. I watched as the men fled from their hellish prison to the banks of the Wiskonset. There they would be guided by their Spirit and carried by the current on large bark rafts until they reached the seclusion of the forest, where they could embark on their quest for freedom. Calvin was right. The diversion he spoke of was a miraculous paradigm of God's intervention. I thought of all those special messengers that had crossed my path to aide this mission. I sat back, closed my eyes, and listened to the hum of the jet motors. *Thank You Lord*, I prayed. *All praise and honor and glory are Yours.*

"One more thing, Andy. Truly saving mankind belongs to the Lord."

I turned to look out the window. *Change starts with the Spirit inside me*, I thought. *I have to be willing to fully submit to His calling. I have to truly trust and believe.* A tear fell as I thanked God for loving me so much. I thanked God for allowing me to be His child and to serve Him and for all His wondrous blessings. I prayed for our journey ahead and for our strength, courage and understanding to discern and obey His commands. I thanked God for delivering us from our oppressors. I prayed for a safe journey for the released prisoners, and that they too would all come to know the Lord and serve Him well. I understood that Jesus would never leave me. I understood that whatever God gives you is yours, and no one can take it away. And I was beginning to understand that as part of the family of God, I also needed to accept my-self as a child of true worth. Stumbling blocks will always try to make you fall, but faith in God conquerors all, and my faith will always prevail beyond the shadows. I looked at the necklace that my father had given me and once again read the message inside. 'Seek Love, Joy, Peace, Patience, Kindness, Goodness, Faithfulness, Gentleness, and Self-Control'. I noticed the word 'Faithfulness' had turned gold while the other words remained silver engravings. I turned to Tommy.

"Look at this. What do you make of it?" I asked.

Tommy carefully examined the words inside the delicate cross. "Do you know what your name means, Andy? Angeleigh means messenger and Aman means to be faithful, endure, trust and believe." He touched the delicate inscription within the cross. "Perhaps you have begun to understand true faith."

I nodded in acknowledgement. "I certainly understand that when you're blessed, it's not only intended for you, but through you, it is to touch so many others as well."

It gave me peace to know we were part of God's royal family. So long had I searched for my parents, so long had I prayed for God to reunite my family. And now God was showing me that family meant all His children. Thinking about this, I wondered how grandmom was doing.

"Dad," I asked, "do you think we'll be able to see Nana soon? I know she must be very worried about me. And you'll come too, won't you, Dad?"

My father turned to me. His face was strong and powerful. He was wise and purposeful. A man with true vision and calling. I was so proud to be his daughter.

"Of course, my dear," my father said as he stared deeply into my eyes. "Together, forever, my dear Angeleigh," he said.

And then a chill, a bone-chilling chill went through every inch of my body as his eyes turned dark, soulless.

This was not my father.

The end. Well, for now.

God Has A Special Plan For You

"For we are God's workmanship, created in Christ Jesus to do good works, which God prepared in advance for us to do." Ephesians 2:10

Give your heart to Jesus

"I am the gate; whoever enters through Me will be saved." John 10:9

Study God's Word

"For everything that was written in the past was written to teach us, so that through endurance and the encouragement of the Scriptures we might have hope." Romans 15:4

Become New in Christ Jesus

"Do not conform any longer to the pattern of this world, but be transformed by the renewing of your mind. Then you will be able to test and approve what God's will is – His good, pleasing and perfect will." Romans 12:2

Pray for guidance

"Show me Your ways, O Lord, teach me Your paths; guide me in Your truth and teach me, for You are God my Savior, and my hope is in You all day long." Psalm 25:4,5

Be steadfast in prayer

"Be joyful always; pray continually; give thanks in all circumstances, for this is God's will for you in Christ Jesus." I Thessalonians 5:16

Develop your gifts

"We have different gifts, according to the grace given us." Romans 12:6

Be patient in your blessing

"But those who hope in the Lord will renew their strength. They will soar on wings like eagles; they will run and not grow weary, they will walk and not be faint." Isaiah 40:31

Be strong in faith

"Now faith is being sure of what we hope for and certain of what we do not see. " Hebrews 11:1

Follow His laws

"Do not let this Book of the Law depart from your mouth; meditate on it day and night, so that you may be careful to do everything written in it. Then you will be prosperous and successful." Joshua 1:8

Know God's power

"Be strong in the Lord and in His mighty power. Put on the full armor of God so that you can take your stand against the devil's schemes. For our struggle is not against flesh and blood, but against the rulers, against the authorities, against the powers of this dark world and against the spiritual forces of evil in the heavenly realms." Ephesians 6:10-12

Share your gift with others

"Each one should use whatever gift he has received to serve others, faithfully administering God's grace in its various forms." I Peter 4:10

Give all praise and glory to God

"Let everything that has breath praise the Lord." Psalm 150:6

SCRIPTURE REFERENCES IN TEXT

SCRIPTURE REFERENCES CITED WITHIN the text :

1 Psalm 46:1 NIV *"God is our refuge and strength, an ever-present help in trouble."*

2 2 Timothy 3: 2-5 NIV *"People will be lovers of themselves, lovers of money, boastful, proud, abusive, disobedient to their parents, ungrateful, unholy, without love, unforgiving, slanderous, without self-control, brutal, not lovers of the good, treacherous, rash, conceited, lovers of pleasure rather than lovers of God- having a form of godliness but denying its power. Have nothing to do with them."*

3 Mark 5:36 NIV *"Don't be afraid; just believe."*

4 Matthew 11:28 NIV *"Come to me, all you who are weary and burdened, and I will give you rest."*

5 Philippians 4:8 NIV *"Whatever is true, whatever is noble, whatever is right, whatever is pure, whatever is lovely, whatever is admirable, if anything is excellent or praiseworthy- think about such things."*

6 Philippians 4:13 NIV *"I can do everything through Him who gives me strength."*

7 Galatians 5:16 NIV *"Live by the Spirit."*

8 Galatians 5:22-23 NIV *"But the fruit of the Spirit is love, joy, peace, patience, kindness, goodness, faithfulness, gentleness, and self-control."*

9 Proverbs 1:33 NIV *"Whoever listens to Me will live in safety*

and be at ease, without fear of harm. "

10Hebrews 12:2 NIV - *"Let us fix our eyes on Jesus, the author and perfecter of our faith. "*

11 Hebrews 11:1 NIV *"Now faith is being sure of what we hope for and certain of what we do not see. "*

12 Hebrews 13:2 NIV *"Do not forget to entertain strangers, for by so doing some people have entertained angels without knowing it. "*

13 2 Thessalonians 3:5 NIV *"May the Lord direct your hearts into God's love and Christ's perseverance. "*

14 1 Peter 1:7 NIV *"Faith – of greater worth than gold."*

15 Romans 8:31 NIV *"If God is for us, who can be against us?"*

CHAPTER HEADING SCRIPTURE REFERENCES

CHAPTER ONE : *"THEREFORE I tell you, whatever you ask for in prayer, believe that you have received it, and it will be yours."* Mark 11:24 NIV

Chapter Two : *"Do not forget to entertain strangers, for by so doing some people have entertained angels without knowing it.."* Hebrews 13:2 NIV

Chapter Three : *"We are hard pressed on every side, but not crushed; perplexed, but not in despair..."* 2 Corinthians 4:8 NIV

Chapter Four : *"Wait for the Lord; be strong and take heart and wait for the Lord."* Psalm 27:14 NIV

Chapter Five : *"He stretches out the heavens like a tent and lays the beams of His upper chambers on their waters. He makes the clouds His chariot and rides on the wings of the wind."* Psalm 104: 2-3 NIV

Chapter Six : *" 'No eye has seen, no ear has heard, no mind has conceived what God has prepared for those who love Him' - but God has revealed it to us by His Spirit."* 1 Corinthians 2: 9-10 NIV

Chapter Seven : *"Be joyful in hope, patient in affliction, faithful in prayer."* Romans 12:12 NIV

Chapter Eight : *"Now faith is being sure of what we hope for and certain of what we do not see. "* Hebrews 11:1 NIV

Chapter Nine : *"You will be secure, because there is hope; you will look about you and take your rest in safety."* Job 11:18 NIV

Chapter Ten : *"In God I trust; I will not be afraid. What can man do to me?"* Psalm 56:11 NIV

Chapter Eleven : *"Are not all angels ministering spirits sent to serve those who will inherit salvation?"* Hebrews 1:14 NIV

Chapter Twelve *: "We live by faith, not be sight."* 2 Corinthians 5:7 NIV

Chapter Thirteen : *"You, O Lord, keep my lamp burning; my God turns my darkness into light."* Psalm 18:28 NIV

Chapter Fourteen : *"Delight yourself in the Lord and He will give you the desires of your heart."* Psalm 37:4 NIV

Chapter Fifteen : *"Death and Destruction are never satisfied."* Proverbs 27:20 NIV

Chapter Sixteen : *"The weapons we fight with are not the weapons of the world."* 2 Corinthians 10:4 NIV

Chapter Seventeen - *"Love must be sincere. Hate what is evil; cling to what is good."* Romans 12:9 NIV

Chapter Eighteen : *"Be strong and courageous. Do not be afraid or terrified because of them, for the Lord your God goes with you; He will never leave you nor forsake you."* Deuteronomy 31:6 NIV

Chapter Nineteen : *"The night is nearly over; the day is almost here. So let us put aside the deeds of darkness and put on the armor of light."* Romans 13:12 NIV

Chapter Twenty : *"You will be secure, because there is hope; you will look about you and take your rest in safety."* Job 11:18 NIV

Chapter Twenty-One : *"You will keep in perfect peace him whose mind is steadfast, because he trusts in You."* Isaiah 26:3 NIV

Chapter Twenty-Two : *"Peace I leave with you; My peace I give you. I do not give to you as the world gives. Do not let your hearts be troubled and do not be afraid."* John 14:27 NIV

Chapter Twenty-Three : *"If you make the Most High your dwelling, even the Lord who is my refuge – then no harm will befall you, no disaster will come near your tent."* Psalm 91: 9-10 NIV

Chapter Twenty-Four : *"A righteous man may have many troubles, but the Lord delivers him from them all."* Psalm 34:19 NIV

Chapter Twenty-Five : *"The Lord will guide you always; He will satisfy your needs in a sun-scorched land and will strengthen your frame."* Isaiah 58:11 NIV

Chapter Twenty-Six : *"Great peace have they who love Your law, and nothing can make them stumble."* Psalm 119:165 NIV

Chapter Twenty-Seven : *"I will save you; you will not fall by the sword but will escape with your life, because you trust in Me, declares the Lord."* Jeremiah 39:18 NIV

Chapter Twenty-Eight : *"The Lord is good, a refuge in times of trouble. He cares for those who trust in Him..."* Nahum 1:7 NIV

Chapter Twenty-Nine : *"The Lord sets prisoners free."* Psalm 146:7 NIV

Chapter Thirty : *"Come to Me, all you who are weary and burdened, and I will give you rest."* Matthew 11:28 NIV

Chapter Thirty-One : *"Be self-controlled and alert."* 1 Peter 5:8 NIV

Chapter Thirty-Two : *"Do not be deceived: God cannot be mocked."* Galatians 6:7 NIV

Chapter Thirty-Three : *"He brought them out of darkness and the deepest gloom and broke away their chains."* Psalm 107:14 NIV

Chapter Thirty-Four : *"...being confident of this, that He who began a good work in you will carry it on to completion until the day of Christ Jesus."* Philippians 1:6 NIV

STUDY AND DISCUSSION QUESTIONS

I. In *FAITH BEYOND the Shadows*, the main character Angeleigh loves the Lord. She reads and studies her cherished Word of God - the Bible and has been raised in the loving and Godly home of her grandmom all her life. Yet there is a deep emptiness in her that consumes her thoughts as well as her perception of herself, keeping her from experiencing the fullness of God's blessings and the peace that Christ offers. She has an unending need to find her long-lost parents and a burning in her heart to help others on a major scale. God, our Father, wants us to be joyful and receive every gift He has in store for us. He knows our needs even before we do and He wants us to depend on Him. As we learn with every good relationship in life, our connection to God requires time spent in fellowship with Him.

Question- What keeps you from experiencing the fullness of God? Here are some Scripture points to guide you- Read: Jeremiah 1:5; Psalm 1:2-3; Psalm 119.

2. Fear and doubt are Angeleigh's constant companions throughout the story. They try to stop her from keeping her focus on the Lord and her mission, and from attaining peace. Only as the story nears the end does she begin to exercise her faith over fear and realize that God has given her all she needs to succeed and fulfill her calling.

Question- What negative characteristics follow you around and try to prevent you from accomplishing your mission? Here are some Scripture points to guide you-Read: On laziness - Proverbs 10:4; On fear - Hebrews 13:6; On seeking worldly approval - I John 3:1; On greed - I Peter 5: 2-3; On doubt - Matthew 21:21; On lust to do other things - I John 2:15-17. (There are many more Scripture verses you may find yourself by using a Concordance.)

3. The spirits that Angeleigh met in the clouds gave her a mission that would ultimately answer her life's prayer to be with her parents and to help others by strengthening her relationship with God and by trusting Him completely. They told her she must tell others to believe but in order to spread such a message to others with conviction, she needed to be a true believer herself. As her faith grew increasingly throughout the story, she began to understand one of the many gifts of the Holy Spirit–faithfulness.
Question- What has God given you to do that requires you to take that leap of faith? Here are some Scripture points to guide you-Read: Romans 12:6-8; I Corinthians 12:4-11; Philippians 4:13. Research more on your own.

4. In the story, other people were put in strategic positions to aid Angeleigh's mission- her father, her grandfather, Lady Maggie, Kyra, Calvin, etc. To avoid famine in Egypt, God placed Joseph in the very strategic position as Chief Magistrate. God placed Daniel in a position to interpret Nebuchadnezzar's dreams which ultimately showed him the sin of pride and that without God, he was helpless. He was a bad king to his people, but was humbled after years in the desert and he repented. The Bible tells of many such truths that are just as applicable today as they were in Bible times and throughout history.
Question- Looking back on your life, can you recall instances when God has placed others in your path to help you to the next step and

to exercise the courage to do God's will? Here are some Scripture points to guide you- the Book of Daniel; the story of Joseph-Genesis 37-50.

5. When her grandfather dies and she questions her father's honesty, Angeleigh wonders if she'll ever be with her parents even though the cloud people have told her that they are required to complete her mission. Discouragement is a powerfully negative emotion. We all get discouraged but we can trust that God will see us through the rough times and so He tells us to not grow weary, but instead to seek the Lord in all that we do.

Question -How do you fight discouragement? Here are some Scripture points to guide you -Galatians 6:9; Hebrews 6: 10-12. Research more on your own.

MAP OF REGION #22

ANGELEIGH'S NEIGHBORHOOD

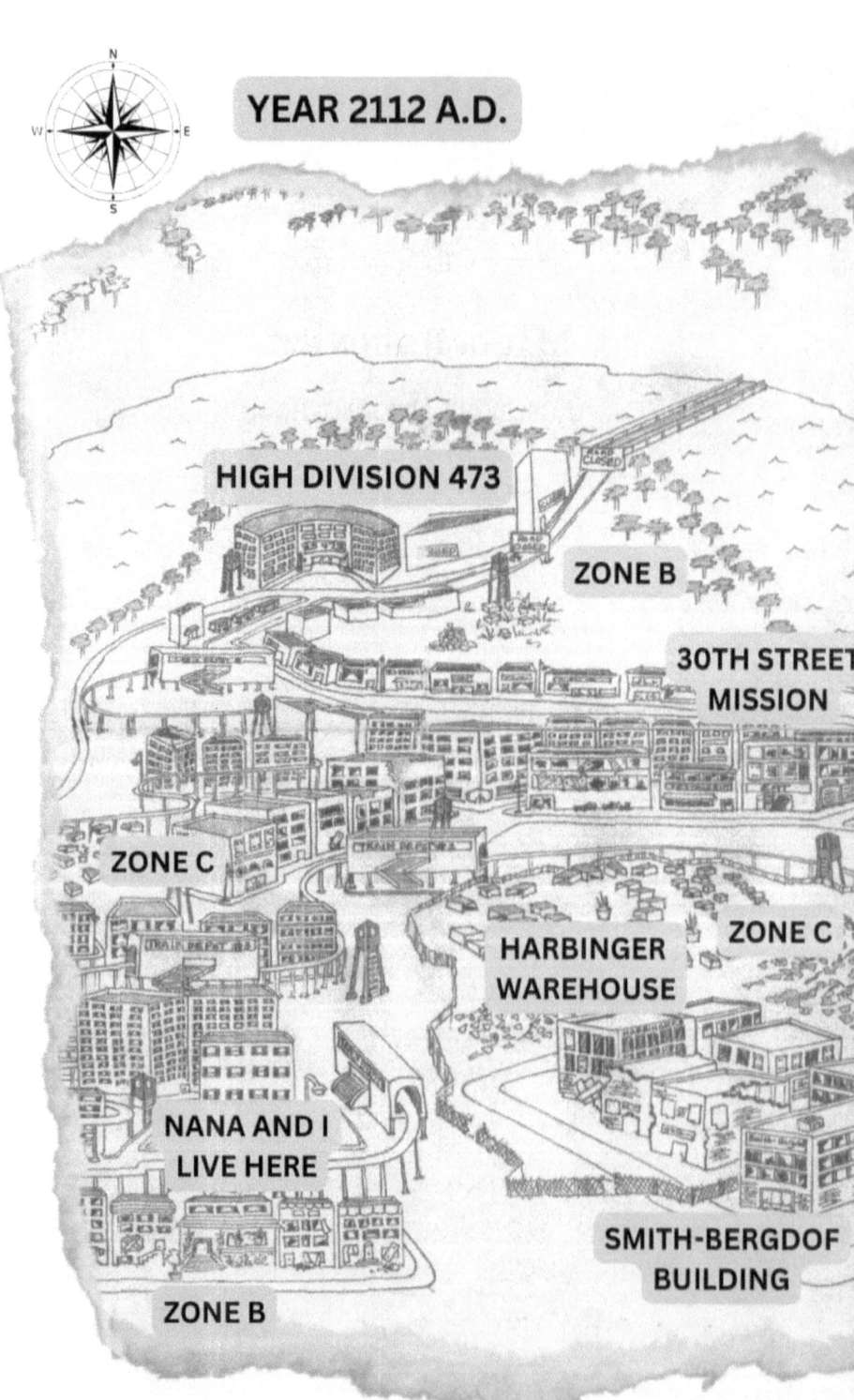

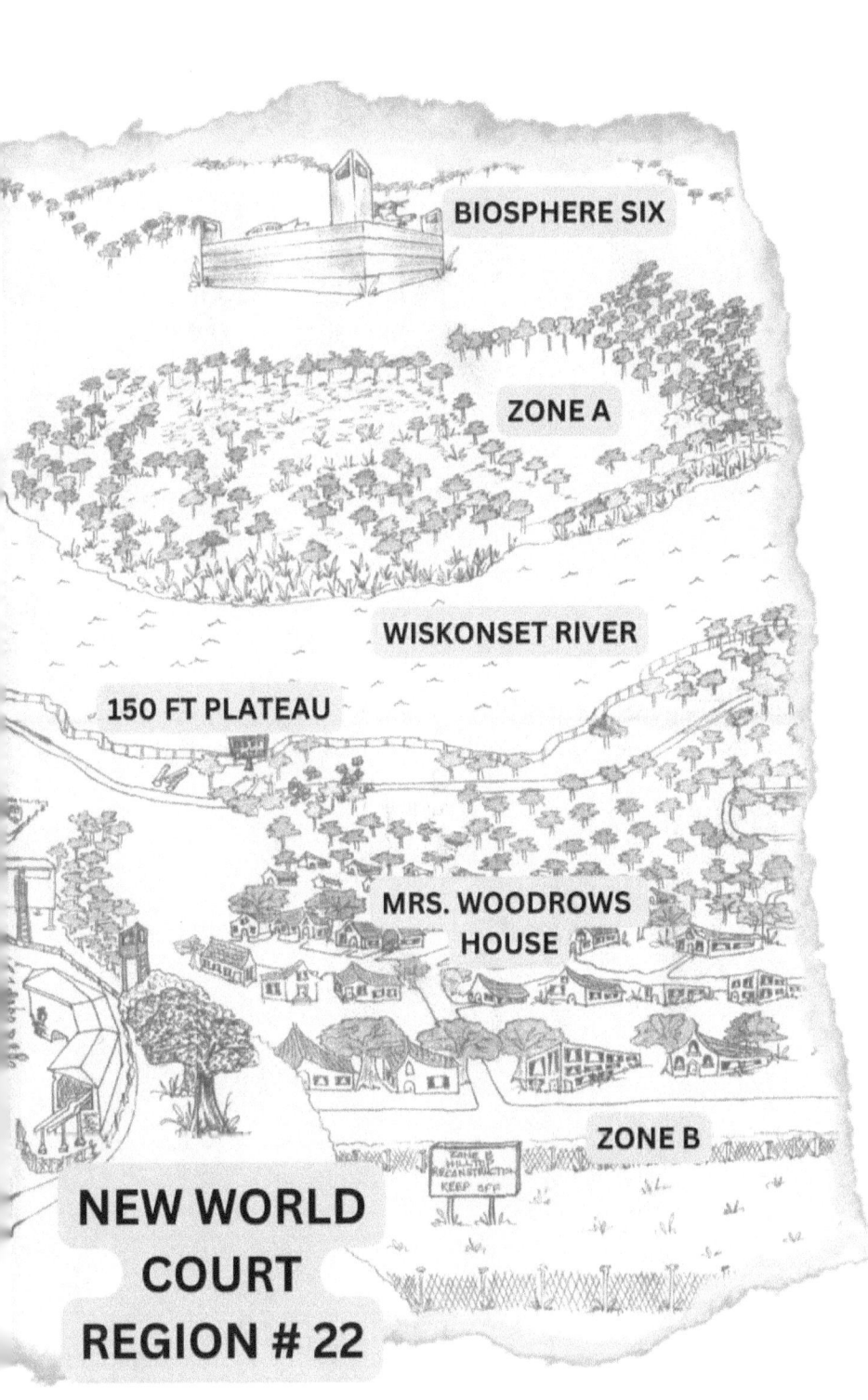

BIOSPHERE SIX

ZONE A

WISKONSET RIVER

150 FT PLATEAU

MRS. WOODROWS
HOUSE

ZONE B

**NEW WORLD
COURT
REGION # 22**

About the Authors

Charlene and Leon Campfield Sr are co-authors of Christ-centered books for young people. They enjoyed almost forty years of marriage before Leon passed on to his heavenly resting place. Throughout their marriage, they raised two beautiful children who went on to be a part of their band, The Campfield Experience. Their music was self-taught and their songs were self-written. Their genre was inspirational rock, jazz and blues. Leon was the lead drummer and lead singer. His vocal range was tenor to bass and his voice had a heavenly echo that reflected his love for Christ. Charlene played lead and rhythm guitar and sang backup. She wrote the lead sheets and kept the business part of the band in order. Jasmine was the second drummer and backup singer. She was a natural. Since the day she sat down at the drums, she never missed a beat. She was fast and fluid, her rhythm was uncompromising. Jamie was an unbelievable bass player. His creative ability was nothing short of amazing, developing his own techniques and carrying the rhythms into uncharted territories. He also sang backup, filling in the three-part back-up harmony. Over the twenty three years that they played, they have many memories to reflect on.

Charlene now operates Campfield and Campfield Publishing LLC, a Christian Indie Publishing company that produces titles for children, teens and young adults. Their mission is to encourage young people to further God's Kingdom for His glory through the generous gifts He gives to each of us. Of their titles, their children's picture books reflect their journey in music.

Charlene also operates Campfields Learning LLC, a Christian Resource webstore that has been redesigned to not only include Bibles and Christian Books but also publications concerning healthy cooking, sustainability, homeschool, school supplies, missions, biographies, and other related Christian works.

ABOUT CAMPFIELD AND CAMPFIELD PUBLISHING

Campfield and Campfield Publishing began in 2009 as a Global Initiative for Christ-Centered Communications. Our goal through our publications is to encourage young people to use their talents to further God's Kingdom for His glory. We have all been given a special gift from God to develop and to share with others. Whatever God has given you to do, He will guide you through it. Pray, have faith, be diligent, be thankful, persevere through the rough times, believe through all times. Always keep the promises of God in your heart.

Remember - "You can do all things through Christ Who strengthens you." Philippians 4:13

And so it is our mission to bring awareness to God's children that He loves them and desires them to be bold and go forth with His message of love, using the gifts He has given each one of us to work with. You may be a writer, a teacher, in public service, a farmer, a doctor, a leader, a servant...

Whatever you do, DO IT FOR HIS GLORY, and do it well!

"Whatever He says to you to do, do it." John 2:5 and

"Don't be afraid, just believe." Mark 5:36

[A portion of the proceeds from the sales of our books, go to help needy children worldwide.]

Titles Available from

Campfield and Campfield Publishing

Faith Beyond the Shadows
Book 1 of the Believe series
978-0-9817025-6-8 Paperback
978-0-9817025-7-5 eBook

When It All Began
The Prequel to the Believe series
979-8-9885996-0-9

PRAIZIN His Name
A His Kids Adventure
for Ages 4-6
978-0-9817025-4-4 Paperback
978-0-9817025-5-1 eBook

We're All God's Children
A His Kids Adventure
for Ages 4-6
978-0-9817025-0-6 Paperback

So You Think You're Not Important!
Are You Kidding?
A Bible Study for the Mis-Informed
978-0-9817025-9-9

CREDITS

Scripture taken from the HOLY BIBLE, NEW INTERNA-TIONAL VERSION®

Copyright © 1973,1978,1984 by International Bible Society.

Used by permission of Zondervan Publishing House. All rights reserved.

The "NIV" and "New International Version" trademarks are registered in the United States Patent and Trademark Office by International Bible Society. Use of either trademark requires the permission of International Bible Society

Word meanings researched in Vine's Complete Expository Dictionary of Old and New Testament Words by W. E. Vine, Merrill F. Unger, and William White Jr. Thomas Nelson Publishers, Nashville, TN, Copyright ©1984, 1996.

Wind Beneath My Wings - Written by Larry Henley and Jeff Silbar 1982

Precious Lord - Lyrics by Tommy Dorsey 1932, Music adapted by Tommy Dorsey from the tune Maitland by George Allen (1812-1877)

Cover design by Charlene Michele Campfield _ using BookBr ush.com software

Interior illustrations by Charlene Michele Campfield _ edited using Canva Pro software

Thank You!

If you've enjoying reading *Faith Beyond the Shadows*, I would appreciate if you would take a minute out of your very busy day to leave a review on the website where you purchased your book. And if you would like a free download of *When It All Began-A Prequel to the Believe Series*, as well as updates on this series, other books and freebies, please visit one of our websites and sign up for our newsletter.

charlenecampfield.com

campfieldslearning.com

campfieldspublishing.com

You can also get your FREE eBOOK here -

https://dl.bookfunnel.com/cuw51l54yf

It will be so nice to hear from you! I am sincerely thankful to all of my readers for their support. God Bless you.

SPREAD GOD'S LOVE!

"I will never leave you nor forsake you."
Joshua 1:5

CAMPFIELD AND CAMPFIELD
PUBLISHING LLC